THE RESORT

BRYCE GIBSON

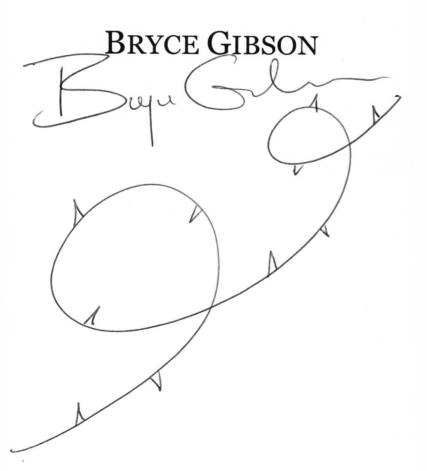

The Resort/Bryce Gibson — 1st edition

ISBN-13: 9781720844846

CHAPTER ONE

WITH AN ISLAND full of teenagers and no internet access, there is the overwhelming sense that all hell is about to break loose.

The resort has one cell phone tower, and it is covered in kudzu. The vigorously growing vine is blocking most of the satellite's signal.

In The South, if gone unchecked, kudzu can get out of hand before you know it. On my trips to the mainland I've seen old school buses, barns, and even acres of forest and farmland completely taken over. People don't call it The Vine That Ate The South for nothing.

I step out of the golf cart and fling the back of the seat forward. Behind the seat is a small storage area where I keep various tools, bottles of water, and what I'm looking for now — a big machete.

Holding the knife in one hand and a sharpener in the other, I run the blade across the flint. The sound is loud in the quiet woods. Once I think the knife is sharp enough, I flick my fingertip across the edge. Yep, sharp as a razor.

Right away, I go to work chopping the kudzu vines off at the ground, and then I pull them loose from the steel risers. Chop, pull, and repeat. It's a rhythm that I easily fall into, and I enjoy it. Doing this, I have a clear-cut goal. Getting rid of the kudzu is something that is attainable.

Then the machete hits something more solid than the tender vines. When I try to raise my arm again, the blade doesn't come loose. It is stuck in whatever I have found. I'm familiar with chopping into thick tree root, and that is exactly what this feels like.

With the knife blade stuck, I let go of the handle and bend over to get a better look. It's a vine that is as thick as my thumb. While crouched down low, I look up. The vine grows skyward and has already begun to wrap itself around the tower.

When I was younger, I would often have nightmares about vines similar to this. In the dreams, the strong tendrils would wrap themselves all around my body, restraining me, making it so I couldn't move. I would wake up terrified, thrashing at tangled bed sheets. Thankfully, I haven't been victim to one of the frightening dreams in a long time.

Whereas the kudzu is growing near the tower's legs, this other vine is coming from somewhere deeper within the woods. I stand, take several steps toward the trees, and stop to look down at my feet. Now I see that there is not only *one* vine—several of them are reaching out from the darkness that looms in front of me.

I step forward and follow the vines several yards into the woods and stop when I hear something moving in the brush ahead of me. There are wild animals on the island, and I know to be on guard. So I grip the machete tighter in my right hand. The sound continues, low to the ground. Something is sliding, rustling through the leaves.

After freaking myself out, I give up on finding the source of the vine and go back to the tower. The whole time that I'm working on clearing the kudzu I keep my eyes focused on the woods. I can't shake the feeling that there is something out there. Something evil that is waiting for its chance to strike.

CHAPTER TWO

AFTER I GET the vines cleared from the cell tower, I'm stuck in Admin all morning. The office is located in a bright yellow cottage that sits at a big curve where the tide marsh cuts deep into the land. From here, I have a clear view of the marina that is on the other side of the inlet water.

When your parents own an island resort, you spend your spring break working, and if the girl you like is on the island for the week, you take full advantage of the opportunity. I'm toggling my laptop screen back and forth between a restaurant supply order and my social media accounts. Kristen, the girl I like, has an online blog that has thousands of followers, and that is where I stop.

Kristen lives in the upstate of South Carolina, near Greenville. I met her last year during spring break when she was here with her older sister, Allison. Kristen and I have kept in touch ever since, and I've even gone to visit her a few times on the mainland. One time, she gave me a silver pendant of two crossed arrows that I put on a leather cord and have worn around my neck every day since. I want to be more than friends, but I haven't told her yet.

I'm reading her latest blog post—one about how she wants to spend her final spring break as a high school student—when the office phone rings. It is Dad calling to remind me that I need to check the safety of the zip line.

After hitting SUBMIT on the supply order, I shut the computer down. As I'm heading out, I peek into Mom's office and remind her that I'm leaving early. She had me scheduled to be in Admin all day and then a shift in the cafeteria tonight, but the zip line has to be checked, and I'm the best at doing it.

All of the work makes for a long day, but it's okay. I have time off that I can spend with Kristen. The thing about working here is the simple fact that my future is set. The island is my legacy. That is, if I *want* it to be.

With being homeschooled on the island for the past four years, I can't stop thinking about what it would be like to have a normal teenage life like everybody else. Even though it is only a thirty minute boat ride to the mainland, sometimes it seems like the water that separates me from them is a million miles wide. Nobody knows it, but there's a stack of college paperwork in my room that's just waiting on my signature. It's a decision I have to make soon— stay here or go off to college in the fall.

I'M GLIDING ALONG the zip line when my cell phone buzzes with an incoming call. I'm forty feet off the ground, and my hands are above my head, grasping the handlebar. Obviously, I can't answer.

We have clear string lights running the length of the course. Right now, in the daylight, the lights are dim. But at night the forest will be lit with the glow from hundreds of amber-colored bulbs.

From this height, I can see some of the landscape patterns of the island. Directly beneath my feet is a tangled mess of running vines, briars, and scattered leaves. Further away, the ocean goes on as far as I can see. Between me and the water, there are the tops of several buildings—three hotels, a barn, and the tin roof of my parents' farmhouse.

Breaking my attention away from the land, I look up. The next platform is directly ahead, and, seconds later, my boots hit the edge of the two-by-fours. Once I'm standing safely on top of the flat surface, I reach into my pocket and pull out my phone. The missed call was from our groundskeeper, Ryan Green. I try to call him back, but phone reception on the island is spotty, and the call doesn't go through.

I pocket the phone and step closer to the

edge. When I lean against the wooden rail, I notice a loose wobble and make a mental note to come back and fix it later. There are several platforms along the zip line's path. This one is built around the trunk of a tall oak tree. From here, I have a pretty good view of the surrounding property. Through the palm and oak trees, I can see our house and yard.

I look just in time to see Ryan making a beeline across the vegetable garden where he'd been working all morning. Obviously he isn't watching where he steps, and I know he is crushing the tender squash and tomato plants that are in his path.

Ryan comes to a stop at the edge of one of the island's three orchards and kneels down. What I see on the ground next to him is a strong punch to the gut. It is something I recognize immediately—my father's bright yellow cap. But it isn't *just* the cap I see—Dad is on the ground too. His body is curled up like he is in pain. Something is wrong. I have to get there. Now.

I jerk back from the rail. Having never bothered to undo myself from the safety harness, the shackle swivels above me when I turn. I step close to the edge of the floor, check the vest to make sure it is secure, and let myself go.

Finally, my feet land on the next platform.

This is one of the starting points of the course, and it is built like a tree house. When I'm steady on my feet, I jerk the vest off and leave it hanging from the line. I charge down the steps and run to where I'd left the golf cart.

After I'm sitting behind the wheel, I fly down the dirt road that cuts through the forest. Following the road all the way will lead to the marina, but I know shortcuts through the land, and I jerk the steering wheel toward an overgrown path on my left. The golf cart bounces over ruts and limbs. The tires come off the ground, but I don't tip over. I land with a thud. The path is rough, but I know it will spit me out right where I want to be.

When I reach the scene, Ryan has Dad pulled tight into his arms, and Dad is clutching the left side of his chest. I wonder if he is having a heart attack, but then I see the blood. Dark red is everywhere. It only takes me a second to realize that the blood is coming from Dad's right hand and forearm. Ryan looks up at me, and I can tell that he is worried. "Help is on the way," he says.

Dad's arm looks like it has been ripped open with sharp claws. I feel like I'm going to either hurl or pass out, so I sit down on the ground. Judging from the amount of blood, it looks like he could bleed to death. "What happened?"

Dad winces at the sound of my voice and mumbles something that I can't comprehend.

"He was messing with that tree," Ryan says and glances toward the barn.

Behind the barn is a small, fenced-in plot of land that is home to a garden of carnivorous plants. Bladderworts, Venus flytraps, pitcher plants, and, in the dead center of it all, stands one of Dad's prized possessions—a Ya-Te-Veo, a man-eating tree.

The tree is about waist high and is several feet in circumference. Truthfully, it's really more of a stump than anything else. From the flat surface of the top, long thorn-covered frond-like leaves stretch all the way to the ground. The leaves kind of remind me of a Century Plant. Or a squid. Or the head of the Lovecraftian monster, Clthulu. People say that the Ya-Te-Veo is able to lift the tendril-y fronds and trap its prey. It crushes the victim and then drains their blood.

According to Dad, the plant in our backyard started as a cutting that came directly from the infamous man-eating tree of Madagascar. Based on accounts from the late 1800s, the Madagascar Tree fed on members of a local tribe called the Mkodos. One report says that the tree resembles a comfy resting spot in the forest, waiting for someone to take a seat. We've never seen the one on the island do anything cool like that, but I know Dad *wants* it to be true.

Dad likes to chase these kinds of plant-based legends. I've been with him to the Florida Everglades in search of the Moss Man and to the vast farmland of West Virginia where we went looking for a creature that only one person claims to have spotted, the Vegetable Man. Dad and I have never seen anything ourselves, but he is determined to prove their existence. Personally, I think it's a bunch of crap.

Ryan tells me that Dad placed a raw T-bone steak on the flat surface of the tree, hoping for a reaction from the plant. Suddenly, one of the fronds moved and began wrapping itself around his forearm. Instinctively, Dad jerked back, and the long thorns sliced his flesh open. Trying to get away from the attack, he tripped and banged his head against one of the large, flat rocks that are around the perimeter of the garden.

"With this kind of head trauma, we shouldn't move him," Ryan tells me.

While sitting on the ground listening to all of this, I wonder if Dad is delusional. I want more than anything for him to accept that all of this stuff is not real. Things like the Ya-Te-Veo are called urban legends for a reason.

Minutes later, the EMTs arrive in a helicopter from the mainland. I stand to the side and watch the chopper land in the open yard. Everything around me stirs with the constant hum of the spinning blades. As soon as the helicopter is grounded, two medics rush out and run to Dad.

Mom is still in the Admin office when all of this happens, but she gets here as quickly as she can. Dad is flown to the hospital on the mainland.

As it turns out, Dad needs stitches in his arm and a heavy dose of meds for a mild concussion. The doctor puts him on bed rest, and Mom and I set up a temporary sleeping arrangement in the sunroom that is located right off the kitchen. In the room, pots of edible and medicinal herbs line the shelves. Dad is sleeping.

"Mackenzie," Mom calls me into the living room. She is sitting on the edge of the sofa. Her painting easel is standing in front of her. "I'm sorry about this." She looks up from the canvas. The painting is of a thistle that has a bright pink bloom and thorny leaves. "I had to shift everybody's schedules around. I hope it doesn't interfere with whatever you and Kristen had planned."

I shrug my shoulders. "We can just hang out after I get off work. She's got Tina to spend time with anyway." This year, instead of her sister, Kristen came to the island with her best friend. "It's fine. I promise."

Since I started working more around the resort, Mom and Dad have been able to spend more time with their hobbies. It wasn't until last summer that Mom finally pulled her painting supplies down from the attic where they had been stored for the past sixteen years.

THE EATERY IS the only restaurant on the island, and it sits on a roundabout where people can park their golf carts and bikes. On each side of the building are large patios that hold tables and chairs. After I pedal my bike there, I spend the next six hours in the kitchen, flipping burgers and cooking fries. It's midnight by the time I get off work.

This late at night, the island is dark. Porch lights and streetlights are prohibited for the safety of nesting sea turtles. The only light is that of the nearly full moon.

The campsite is located at the west end of the island. Once I get to the wooden boardwalk that stretches over the dunes, I get off the bike, lean it against an old piece of driftwood, and walk across the boardwalk.

This year, in addition to the usual tents, there are several yurts that are scattered among the sandy beach. There is power running to the campsite, and some of the campers have strung string lights along the poles and over their tents.

Several people are sitting around a small bonfire that's been lit on the beach. The sound of a strumming guitar mixes with the rhythm of the crashing waves. From here, the people are only silhouettes in the distance, but one of them stands and begins walking toward me. It doesn't take long for me to realize that it is Kristen. Both of us continue walking, and we meet midway. I can tell by the expression on her face that something is wrong.

"I've got to go get Tina," she says and is flipping her phone around in her hands. "She went to a party, and now she's ready to go. You know I *hate* frat parties." Last year, Kristen's sister was kicked out of this same sorority for a slip in her grades. Afterwards, Kristen wrote a blog post about the pressures of sorority life interfering with school work. The blog post went viral. "I guess I'm kind of notorious in their eyes. You'll go with me, right?"

CHAPTER THREE

THE PARTY IS in the nicest of the three hotels on the island.

The Mandevilla sits in the furthest point of a cove that stretches out to the sea. It is surrounded by tall marsh grasses. Normally it is where visiting businessmen and celebrities like to stay. There is room service and a bar that overlooks the marsh. During the off season, The Mandevilla is the only one of the three hotels that we keep open. It is usually a scene of sophistication and relaxation. Tonight there is a girl puking in the marsh grass.

As we are walking past, Kristen steps away from the heaving girl. The barfer is wearing a t-shirt that has the logo of her sorority plastered across the front. Her dark hair is pulled back in a ponytail. A long necklace is around her neck. The weight of the pendant is causing the whole thing to swing back in forth with every gag. I'm about to go over there and offer help, but a stocky guy comes up behind the girl and places his right hand on her back. In his other hand, he is holding a can of beer that he raises to his lips.

I follow Kristen down the crushed shell walkway that leads through the dunes. We round the corner, and the wrought iron gate to the swimming pool stands in front of us. From the other side of the gate, I can hear laughter and then a splash of water. There is the distant sound of music. Normally a room key is required to open the gate, but tonight it is hanging open from where it had been wedged with one of the hotel's plastic ice buckets.

I follow Kristen through, and we round the corner to the back patio. It doesn't take long for me to realize that the horrible music is actually coming from two different speakers.

The pool area is hopping. The tiki bar on the far side of the space is crammed full of people. Every lounge chair around the water is taken. The pool is full of laughing teenagers. Most of them are holding drinks. I follow Kristen around the water to where a fraternity guy is straddling the high dive. He is wearing a cowboy hat that's been made out of cardboard beer cases.

"Hey, Caleb," Kristen yells over the music and steps closer to the edge of the water. Because of Allison's prior involvement with the sorority, Kristen is no stranger to the parties and knows some of the members.

Caleb turns his head to look at her. I can see right away that his eyes are bloodshot.

"Where's Tina?" Kristen asks.

Caleb squints his eyes and looks from Kristen, to me, and back to her. He looks confused. Because of the loud music, he didn't hear the question.

Kristen yells the question louder this time.

Caleb points up, toward the hotel. A blonde girl wades through the water and grabs Caleb's ankle. They start laughing, and she pulls him in. Caleb goes under, and the cowboy hat bobs to the surface.

"What room?" Kristen asks once Caleb breaks the surface, but he ignores her. Now, he and the blonde girl are making out in the water.

Kristen grabs my hand. "Let's go," she says.

With her in the lead, we start walking toward the hotel, and I hear Caleb's voice behind me. "Your boyfriend's not allowed inside," he yells.

Caleb is staring back at me from the water. "Was he talking to us?" I ask Kristen.

"Yeah, but you'll be fine."

The hotel lobby is quiet and gives no indication of the wild frat party that is going on outside. Brenda, the front desk receptionist, looks up at us. Her eyes catch mine, and she gives me a knowing smile before turning her back and walking into the office. I know that she won't tell Mom or Dad that I was there.

Kristen and I step into the elevator, and she pushes the button for the fifth floor. The doors slide shut. When I feel the elevator start to move, I speak up. "Caleb called me your boyfriend," I point out.

"Yeah, he likes to jump to a lot of conclusions."

Before I have a chance to say anything else, the elevator doors open. The fifth floor hallway is stretched out in front of us. Now it is obvious that the night's party wasn't contained to the pool area.

Most of the room doors are standing open, and the hall is full of frat guys and sorority girls. None of them look toward us. They are too caught up in their own conversations.

Inside, the music is different. We're walking down the hall when a frat boy steps in front of us, blocking our path. He looks pissed. It is obvious that we don't belong here, and he has come to do something about it. When he gets closer, he looks at Kristen and smiles. "Holy shit. You're Allison Thomas's little sister," he says. "All grown up…" He eyes her up and down. I can smell the liquor on his breath.

"Where is she?" Kristen blurts out.

The guy shrugs his shoulders. "Who?"

Kristen rolls her eyes. "Tina," she tells him. "I'm taking her with me. Where is she?"

"Oh, you mean the cute little red head?"

Kristen storms past and bumps into the guy's arm. The beer in his cup sloshes out. I start to follow behind her, but the guy puts his hand on the wall, blocking my path. Again, he leans closer to me and shakes his head. "Unless you're part of the fraternity, no dudes allowed."

I look up and see that Kristen is midway down the hall. She is facing my direction. The guy is still blocking my way. Kristen holds up her right hand and has one finger raised. "One minute," she whispers. Then she turns back around and walks away.

The guy shoves me back. "Out. Now," he says.

I feel terrible about leaving Kristen, but I turn around and walk away. When I get to the end of the hallway, I press the button for the elevator. The doors open to reveal a guy and girl making out inside. Neither of them pause to look at me. There's no way I'm getting on the elevator with them, and I let the doors shut. I turn around and crash my body weight into the stairwell door. The lobby is five stories down, but I don't care. I've got to get out of here.

The sound of my feet echoes through the stairwell. There is laughter coming from below. A couple of stories lower, I pass two guys that are wearing fraternity shirts, no doubt headed to where I just came from.

Finally, I push open the door that leads to the lobby, and I go straight to the exit. Once I'm outside, I turn to the left and creep along the perimeter of the building to where I find a sandy path that leads to the ocean.

CHAPTER FOUR

I IGNORE THE signs that say to stay off the dunes and plop myself down in a bare spot in the sand. This is where I'll wait on Kristen. The tall, reedy grasses reach up on each side. The music from the hotel is still going strong. In front of me, the ocean crashes to the shore, and the white moonlight is reflecting off its surface. From somewhere in the distance, I hear a scream that sounds like something from a horror movie. It sends shivers down my spine. I take out my phone and text Kristen, letting her know where I am.

The internet is actually working, and I'm scrolling through my phone when I hear something else. It is the sound of something moving through the dry reeds. I spin around to look, but there's nobody there. Then I hear what is undeniably the sound of someone crying. I get to my feet and stretch my neck, looking around the area. I don't see a soul, but the sound is close.

"Hello?" I call out.

"I didn't know anybody was out here." It is a girl's voice coming through choked-back sobs. Now I see her. She is sitting in the sand not fifteen feet from where I am. In the dark she is hard to see, but now that I know she is there, the moonlight seems to make her blonde hair glow.

I stand up and walk over to her.

"It's been a shitty night for you too?" I ask while I'm standing over her.

She uses the inside of her hand to wipe the tears from her cheeks. "You don't even know the half of it," she tells me and throws a small, crumpled piece of paper into the grass.

"Well, do you mind if I join you?"

She looks up at me and shrugs her shoulders. "Sure. If you want to spend part of your spring break with a cry-baby."

I sit down, and there is a long, awkward silence between the two of us. I kick at the sand, waiting for her to tell me more.

"I should have never come on this stupid trip." She leans forward and wraps her arms around her knees. "Are you one of them?" She turns her head to look at me. Her cheeks are streaked with mascara from when she has been crying.

I don't understand what she is asking at first, and then it hits me—she thinks I'm part of the stupid fraternity. "No," I tell her. "God, no."

"Why are you here then?"

"My parents..."

She nods her head as if understanding and cuts me off. "They wanted you out of the house and sent you here."

Like Caleb, this girl is so bad at making assumptions. "What's your name?" I ask.

"Brockley…"

I start laughing. "Sorry. It's just… Broccoli? Really?"

"Yes, really. And it's not like the vegetable," she spells out her name for me. "You know what's really funny about my name? I'm a botany major."

She's right. It is funny, and I laugh.

"Who are you?"

"Mackenzie," I tell her. "Mackenzie Walker."

Her eyes get really wide. "Your parents own this place."

"Yeah, I was about to tell you that, but…"

"Mackenzie," It's Kristen's voice I hear behind me. I turn to look and see her coming down the sandy dune. Tina is behind her and nearly stumbles over her own feet. Finally, the two of them are standing right behind me. "I've been looking everywhere for you," Kristen says.

I'm already starting to stand. I don't want Kristen to think that me and this Brockley chick were up to anything.

"Brockley Davis?" Kristen says. She is squinting through the darkness to get a clearer look at who I've been talking to.

"What are you doing here?" Brockley asks Kristen. "I didn't think I'd ever see you again after what happened with your sister."

Kristen is about to say something, but there is a second scream. This one is closer—coming from the pool area. All of a sudden, the music stops. Kristen, Tina, and I turn to look at one another and then we go running toward the fence.

By the time we get there, a crowd of spectators has already gathered around the hotel doors. Caleb climbs out of the pool and joins the others. The girl that pulled him into the water is walking with him. The hotel door opens, and the crowd parts. Some of them are holding up their phones, taking pictures of what they see in front of them.

Two heavy-set guys are holding up a third guy between them. Next to the other two, the one in the middle appears too thin, but then I realize that he is actually trim and fit.

"What's going on?" I ask Kristen.

Then the two guys on each end ease the third dude down to the concrete where they let him lie flat on his back. A hush has fallen over the crowd. Another guy pushes his way through and kneels down next to the still body.

The new guy is checking the fallen guy's pulse, and, a second later, he has both of his hands on his chest, pumping up and down. The actions become more urgent, and then he stops. He turns around to look at the crowd, at no one in particular. "He needs an ambulance," he says.

The crowd is quiet. I can tell what they are thinking. We are all thinking the same thing—he's not going to make it.

"Is he dead?" The voice spooks me, and I spin around to be face to face with Brockley. I hadn't realized that she followed us up the embankment. In the moonlight, her eyes look like they are glowing. They are bloodshot from when she has been crying. The shimmering light reflecting from the pool water dances over her face, making her look like a monster.

CHAPTER FIVE

THIS MARKS THE first time someone has died on the island.

After the guy was carried out of the hotel, the resort's security officer, Rebecca Wooley, arrived on the scene and called the paramedics. They transported the guy to the hospital on the mainland, and, less than an hour later, he was pronounced dead.

Later in the night, the pictures circulating social media tell all we need to know. One photo is of a group of three guys standing in a hotel room. I know that it is one of the rooms in The Mandevilla because of the paintings on the wall. Each of the three guys has a belt looped around his neck. From there, the belts are tied to the shelf that's on the wall behind them.

Next, there is a video of the same scene. Here, the guy on the far left goes down, and the weight of his body rips the entire shelf off the wall. The shelf crashes on top of him. There is laughter behind the camera. The video continues until the other two guys pass out, and their knees go slack.

I've heard of the game before. It's called The Choking Game. The object of the game is to strangle yourself or someone else until you or the other player is close to passing out. They say you get a high, a sense of euphoria as the blood rushes back to your brain. The fraternity must have been using the game as a hazing ritual.

If the pressure is not released in time, the game could result in strangulation, causing permanent brain damage. Even death.

I go back to the first photo and click on the names that were tagged in the post until I find who I'm looking for. His name was David Fiske. According to his bio he was nineteen, only two years older than I am now, a simple fact that cuts deep into my heart.

Trying to get the thought to go away, I do a quick scroll through David's photos. But, really, there is nothing on there that stands out big to me. He just looks like a normal guy. Lots of friends. Full of life. Now... dead.

Finally, I turn off my phone and try to sleep. I eventually fall into a fitful slumber, but I dream that I'm one of those idiots playing the stupid game. The belt around my neck is being pulled tighter and tighter by invisible hands, cutting off my airway until everything around me goes hazy and I'm gasping... I reach my hand to the belt, trying to pull it loose, when I catch my reflection in a tall mirror that's on the other side of the room. It's *not* a belt that's wrapped around my neck—it's a thick, green vine.

When I wake, the sun is shining through the window. This is the first dream that I've had about one of the vines in a long time, and it leaves me feeling unsettled. The vines on the cell tower and the idea of The Choking Game have coiled themselves together in my subconscious. I stand from the bed and make my way downstairs. Mom is in the kitchen. She is at the counter, pouring herself a cup of coffee. The kitchen table is cluttered with paperwork, and the chair on the far end is sitting cattycorner. I know she has been up early working. Mom steps away from the coffee pot and places the mug down on the table. "You're going to have a busy day," she tells me. "Most of The Mandevilla is vacating."

What she is saying doesn't surprise me. I mean, who would want to stay in a hotel where someone has just died? Without warning, the image of David Fiske's smiling face flashes through my mind. Behind me, two pieces of bread pop up from the toaster. The sound scares the beejeezus out of me, and I jump.

"The toast is for you." Mom nods her head in my direction.

I spin around so that I'm facing the

counter. I get the toast and begin slathering gobs of butter and apricot jam on top of each piece with the closest thing I can find, a large butcher knife. I'm assigned to work at The Bike Shed this morning, and I know it's going to be crazy with everybody trying to get out.

When I turn around, Mom is gathering the paperwork. "Give them a full refund on their bikes," she tells me. "I'll be busy trying to smooth things over with PR."

As I bite into the first piece of toast, I glance over Mom's shoulder toward the sunroom. Dad has moved to the chair in the corner. Holding his phone, he dials a number and then presses the phone to his ear.

"If you have any problems, give me a call," Mom tells me and waves her phone in the air. The coffee mug is in her other hand, and a thick binder is under her right arm. She pushes the swinging door open with her rear.

After I'm left alone in the kitchen, I go to the fridge and grab a carton of OJ. The carton is almost empty, so I take the whole thing with me. I sit on top of the table where I finish my toast and guzzle the last of the juice. When I'm done with breakfast, I head upstairs and get dressed.

Outside, it is already sunny and warm. There is not a cloud in the sky. It is a beautiful day—perfect, even—but I know that it is deceiving.

On the way to The Bike Shed, I pass by the largest flower garden on the island. The plot of land is broken up into quadrants of evergreens and tropical blooms. There is a girl in the far back corner standing next to a large carrion flower. Out of all of the plants on the island, it is this one that gets the most attention. It is commonly called a corpse flower because of the open bloom's smell—that of decaying flesh. The corpse flower rarely opens, and the flower lasts twenty-four to thirty-six hours before collapsing in on itself.

The girl stands up straight, and I realize that it is Brockley. She has a clipboard in her hand. We wave at each other, but I don't slow down.

What a weirdo, I think. What college student would come to a tropical island for spring break and spend her time studying and taking notes?

By the time that I pull my bike up to the marina, it is already a scene of chaos and mayhem. People are stumbling around zombie-like, still hung over from the night before. After I get off my bike, I'm pushed out of the way by a girl with an enormous piece of luggage. The suitcase appears to be big enough to carry a dead body.

"Move," she says. "I've got to get off this island."

I twirl around to get out of her way and notice that she is holding a phone in her right hand.

"There's no wi-fi," she says. "This place is a *nightmare*!" She storms past me without a second glance and pushes her way through the rest of the crowd to where she heaves the bag into the waiting boat.

The statement about there being no wi-fi strikes me as strange. I just cleared off the tower yesterday morning—the signal should be fine.

I go into The Bike Shed and unlatch the sides, one at a time. The hinges are on the bottom of the panels, and I let each of the flaps free-fall to where they crash against the interior wall.

On the other side of the open window, the crowd of impatient college students are waiting on me. Most of them are holding their phones. They wear faces of disbelief. Eyes bloodshot. I wave the first customer over.

The girl steps forward. With her hands on her hips, she scrunches her nose and looks around at her surroundings. "What's that awful smell?"

"Pluff mud," I tell her.

The odor comes from the thick mud around the edge of the water. It *is* pungent, but I guess you get used to it.

"Name?" I ask the girl. She answers, and I go to the filing cabinet to pull her rental agreement. Then I step back to the counter and give the waiting girl her refund. After she wanders away, the next customer comes forward. I repeat this process all morning until the first boatload of passengers departs to the mainland.

I brought my lunch—a PB&J sandwich and a bag of chips—and I'm able to take bites in between helping the group that will be boarding the next boat out of here. While I'm flipping through the folder, I accidentally drop the whole thing, and the papers scatter across the concrete floor.

I bend over and begin picking up my mess, and, as soon as I stand up straight, I see Mom walking down the boardwalk toward me. Just the fact of seeing her here I immediately know something is wrong. Mom *never* comes to the marina.

By the time I have the pages back in a neat stack, Mom has already entered the shed and is standing beside me. "Your dad went to Trenton," she says.

While Mom and I have been working this morning, Dad must have taken the small private boat that he keeps moored at one of the inlets closer to the house.

Mom continues. "He left a note, saying there was somebody in town he needed to talk to. He's convinced that what happened last night has something to do with Silas Harrow."

"Silas Harrow? Really?" I can't believe he is blaming what happened to David Fiske on something as ludicrous as an old urban legend.

According to the story, Silas was found hanging from the limb of a big oak tree back in 1800s. They say he haunts the fields around the small town. Here, on the island, David Fiske died from playing a game. There's even video proof.

By now, I've finally found the paper I was looking for, and I move to the cash register where I begin processing the customer's refund.

"None of my calls are going through. What if something's wrong with him?" Mom asks.

There are two things that the question makes me think of—blood and feathers. When I was little, probably around five or six, I watched a car crash into a chicken truck. I remember seeing a wing flapping against the bloody asphalt. That image has never left my mind. It pops up at unexpected times. Like last Christmas when the downy feathers on the back of our angel tree topper made me think of death.

"Somebody's got to go find him," I say. "Dad's concussed and on medication. It's not safe for him to be driving and wandering around on his own. He could have hallucinations or... something *worse* could happen." At the thought of the grave danger he could be in, I swallow the lump that has formed in my throat. "I'll do it." I shrug my shoulders. "After I'm done here, I'll see if Kristen will go with me."

CHAPTER SIX

TYLER ADDISON COMES in to work not long after the boat has left.

"Man," Tyler says. "You should see the cell tower. That thing is completely covered in these crazy looking vines…"

Tyler is a short, scruffy dude with a hairstyle that faintly resembles a mullet. Usually, like now, he is wearing a trucker cap.

"What do you mean?" I ask, cutting him off. "I cleared it yesterday. There's no way it's grown back already."

Tyler holds up his hands in defense. "I'm just telling you what I saw, man."

After I finish verifying my register for the shift change, I jump on my bike and begin to pedal away from the marina. I assume that Kristen will be laying out on the beach with Tina. The fastest route to get there is by cutting through the woods which will also take me right by the cell tower. I can see if what Tyler is saying is true.

Riding my bike down the path through the woods is rough, but I manage to make it all the way to the clearing. When I get there, what I see in front of me is unbelievable. Nearly the whole tower is covered with the thick, woody tendrils of the unknown vine.

From the other side of the tower I see a flash of red. A shirt. I crane my neck so I can get a better look. It is Ryan exiting the small electrical shed behind the tower. Once he's out, Ryan pulls the door closed and wiggles the doorknob. I get off my bike and let it fall to the ground. The sound of the bicycle hitting the thick carpet of leaves causes Ryan to look in my direction.

"Mackenzie," he says. "I didn't think I'd see you out here." Ryan reaches for an ax that is propped next to the wall. With the ax in his hand, he starts walking toward me. "This is something, isn't it?" Ryan asks when we are facing each other. Now, he is looking up at the twisted vegetation.

"What is it?" I ask him.

"I'm not really sure," he tells me. "But with plants like this, you've got to know how to control them or things can get out of hand really quick."

The comment reminds me of a time when Ryan told me about a conspiracy theory that the government placed kudzu in The South as a way to destroy The Bible Belt.

"Vines are invasive," Ryan continues. "In order to thrive, they'll strangle out everything else around them."

Ryan is only a few years older than I am—he's in his early twenties. When he came to the island last year, he was a recovering alcoholic. Several months prior to his arrival, he wrecked his truck. The passenger—his girlfriend—died instantly. Ryan was drunk at the time of the crash. He says being here on the island has helped him heal and to become a different, better person. I glance at the gold cross hanging around his neck. It was a gift from his girlfriend.

"Well, I'm going to get to work on clearing these vines," he tells me.

I leave him there and push my bike the rest of the way through the woods. I emerge to a wide expanse of dunes stretched out in front of me. From here, the ocean isn't visible, but I can hear the crashing waves. I leave my bike next to a wooden swing and then walk down the sandy path that cuts through thick patches of witch-hazel.

Unlit tiki torches are stuck in the sand on the beach. A group of guys are hitting a volleyball back and forth near the water. Between the ball game and where I'm standing, a row of beach chairs are facing the ocean. I spot Tina's unmistakable red hair, and then I see the brunette that is sitting next to her. I go over there.

When I'm in their line of sight, several of the girls look up. From where I'm standing, I can smell the sunblock. Kristen sees me and gets to her feet. She is wearing a bright pink two-piece, and I try not to stare. "You're done with work already?"

I'm not wearing sunglasses, and my eyes are squinting against the bright sunlight. "Dad ran off to Trenton, and I'm going looking for him. Anyway, if you want to go…"

Kristen smiles, biting her bottom lip. "I'm down. Just give me time to change."

THE MARINA IS solemn this late in the afternoon. It is a big change from early this morning.

The floating dock moves gently on the salty water, and the boat is bobbing up and down. The water is unsteady, like a storm may be coming in. Milton, the boat's captain, is already on board, and he waves at us.

Kristen steps in first and takes a seat in the farthest corner. I sit down across from her, and Urchin plops down on the floor between us. Ever since he has been in Milton's care, the old dog hasn't missed a boat ride. Soon I hear the sound of the motor starting, and then I feel the vibrations through my body.

Finally, we begin moving, and I watch the island disappear in the distance. It is like some kind of invisible force is pulling me away, and it feels right.

For thirty minutes, we ride through choppy water until we arrive on the coast of South Carolina near Charleston. The spot where we dock is in a quiet town where Spanish Moss is draped from the tree branches and people paint their doors blue in order to ward off boo-hags.

With money sent by Mom, Milton rents us a car, and Kristen and I set off on our mission of finding Dad.

CHAPTER SEVEN

I FIRST HEARD about Silas Harrow when I was thirteen years old.

Vinyl Prescott and I were standing in Dad's laboratory. Vinyl was a kid that wore unbuttoned long-sleeve flannels over black t-shirts. He had shoulder-length hair and listened to 90s alt-rock. With the combination of the grunge style and the cool name, Vinyl could have been friends with anybody.

Back then I went to a private school on the mainland. It was where I met Vinyl, and the two of us hit it off right away. We would eat lunch outside together every day. Sometimes, Vinyl would spend entire weekends with us on the island.

The laboratory is located behind the main house. The building is made of solid concrete, but the outside has a façade that was built out of old, weathered boards so that it resembles a barn. The look is so accurate that no one would ever guess what's inside.

"C'mon. I want to show you something," I told Vinyl.

Because of pouring rain, the two of us had been in the house all morning, playing video games. By then, we had become restless.

Outside, the rain had finally stopped, and everything glistened with the sparkle of water. Vinyl followed me across the yard where Dad was working in the vegetable garden. Dad looked up at us and waved. "Where are you kids off to?" He used the back of his hand to wipe the sweat from his forehead.

"We're walking down to the creek," I lied.

Dad nodded. "Be careful. That gator's been hanging out around there."

The gator he was talking about was only a foot long and had teeth the size of candy corn. Honestly, I would be surprised if it could eat a mouse.

I led Vinyl toward the woods just like we were headed to the creek, and then I hung a sharp right so that we were standing against the old barn-like building. I peeked around the side and saw that Dad had already gone back to work. I knew with his attention being focused elsewhere, Dad would never know what we were up to.

I pulled the keycard out of my back pocket. "Dad doesn't want anybody going in here," I said and slipped the card into the narrow slot on the top of the door handle. The light on the lock went from red to green, and there was a clicking sound inside the mechanism. I took a deep breath and pushed the door inward.

A long hospital-like hallway stretched out in front of us. There were three doors in the passageway—one on the right, one on the left, and one straight ahead.

"This way," I said and started walking.

A sensor on the wall triggered the overhead fluorescents to come on. After I shut the door, Vinyl followed close behind.

It didn't take long for us to get to the end of the hallway. A set of double doors stood in front of us. There was no lock or anything else to keep us out. I put my hand on the right-side door and pushed.

With me in the lead, Vinyl and I went into the room. The highest point of the "barn's" ceiling was right above us. The sunlight shone in through the glass rooftop. We were standing in the solarium.

Vinyl was looking up, taking it all in.

"You should see it at night," I told him. "The stars and the moon. It's like you're on another planet."

"What *is* all of this?" Vinyl asked me.

Dad's plant specimens were all around us. Some of the plants were so tall that they towered over the two of us. A few were blooming, while others looked like they could pop open any minute.

"He's really into this stuff, huh?" Vinyl asked.

"You haven't even seen the best of it yet," I promised.

I started walking up a slight ramp that wrapped itself around the octagon shaped room. We circled behind the potted plants and ended up on a small platform that had rails on all four sides. On the stainless steel counters were pallets full of small plants in various stages of growth.

"What does he do with all of them?" Vinyl asked me.

"He's making new species," I told him.

It was true. A long time ago, Dad created a hybrid squash plant that is completely resistant to downy mildew *and* squash vine borers. It was how he made all of his money.

"Take a look at this," I told Vinyl. "This is what I wanted you to see."

I stepped over to a wall that was full of diagrams and writings. There were illustrations of several plant-based cryptids—a Cactus Cat, a Leshy, the Honey Island Swamp Monster, and the Vampire Vine. A huge map of the United States was tacked to the wall next to the pictures, and yellow push-pins marked the locations of the sightings.

"Those things aren't real," Vinyl said, talking about the cryptids.

"Dad thinks they are." I was staring at the last picture, The Vampire Vine. On the illustration, a thorny tendril was wrapped around a screaming girl. Out of all of them, the Vampire Vine had always been the one that scared me the most and gave me nightmares. Even then I was imagining the terror of being wrapped in those tendrils, unable to move...

"And Silas Harrow?" Vinyl asked from behind me.

I'd never heard the name before, and I turned around. Vinyl was holding a spiral-bound notebook. He spun the book so that it was facing me.

On the top right, the words *Silas Harrow* were printed in Dad's sloppy handwriting. I took the notebook from Vinyl and flipped through the pages. On one of the first pages was a sketch of a man standing in front of a tree. The man was wearing old-timey looking trousers, a long sleeve shirt, and suspenders. His arms were held straight down by his sides, and where the fingers should have been were long, thin branches.

While I was looking at the book, I could

hear Vinyl moving about behind me. "Um, Mackenzie," he said. "What is this?"

I closed the notebook and stepped over to where Vinyl was standing. He was holding a thick black curtain to the side. It was dark and shadowy on the other side, but I could see a chair that looked like it belonged in a hospital. There were straps and wires that led to some sort of control box on the floor.

What we saw that day spooked both of us, and Vinyl never came back to the island. My social life at school quickly fell apart. Vinyl and I never talked again, and I was left to eat lunch by myself. Then the rumors started. The other kids started saying they heard from Vinyl that Dad was doing experiments with plants *and* humans.

Vinyl told all of them that Dad was making a monster.

Chapter Eight

DESPITE THE NO SMOKING DECAL on the dash, the rental CAR smells like stale cigarette smoke. The smell has been masked by a horrible air freshener that only makes the odor that much more disgusting. Both of us have our windows cracked, letting in some fresh air, hoping to get rid of the funk.

By now, we have been on the road for an hour. Since there's no interstate in the vicinity between us and Trenton, we've been traveling down rural roads that cut through various small towns. The air in this part of the state is considerably cooler than it was back on the resort. I remind myself that it is only April, and the Southern temperature is prone to dip down to freezing during early spring.

"So, tell me about this Silas Harrow character," Kristen finally says.

I take a second to let the story gather in my mind, and then I tell her all I know. "People say that Silas is out there in the peach field where he was hung. He has long, pliable branches for fingers…"

"And let me guess… he wraps the fingers around the victim's neck and strangles him."

I nod. "It must be why Dad thinks David

Fiske's death has something to do with Silas." I roll my eyes at the absurdity of what I'm saying. "But I have no idea why he thinks Silas would have come all the way to the resort."

"Is it common for him to run off like this?"

"He's *never* done it," I tell her. "Honestly, I'm worried about him."

"Does he still have family in Trenton?"

I shake my head. "His sister died when she was little, and his parents are both gone."

We travel in silence for several miles. Being alone with Kristen, I want to tell her how I want to be more than friends, but the time is not right. I should be worried about Dad, not the two of us.

"Well, I think it's great your dad believes in this kind of stuff."

What she says kind of confuses me. "You do?"

"Yeah. I mean, my parents don't believe in *anything* that they can't see with their own eyes."

It's been a long time since I've had a bite to eat, and my stomach makes a loud grumble. Kristen says she could eat too, and we decide to grab something quick in the next town we come to.

There's not much here, just a couple of fast food joints. We pull through the closest drive-through and are back on the road within minutes.

It's been a long time since I've had food from one of the major fast food chains, and it tastes phenomenal. As we eat our burgers and fries, the landscape changes the further we go. The stretch of highway that we're on is full of farmland, old houses, and produce stands. It is so different from what I'm used to on the island. Instead of sand, the surrounding land is made of deep-brown dirt and red clay.

It's nearly dusk by the time we pass by an old, oily looking gas station and finally get to the *Welcome to Trenton* sign. The small town is nothing but a large green park, a post office, lots of old houses, the gas station, and a few abandoned buildings. The area is small, and I hope that we can find Dad by simply driving around.

The last time I'd been here was a long time ago. Back then, I'd come to visit my grandparents, who have both been dead by at least a decade at this point. I think I'll be able to recognize enough of my surroundings from my previous visits to be able to find the spot where Silas was supposedly hanged.

The fields intersect each other, and we can't see any clear divisions in the land. After traveling back and forth over the same stretch of road, the car's low-fuel light comes on. I turn the car around and head back to the old gas station.

After pulling up to the outdated pump, I get out of the car. There is not a slot for debit cards. I glance toward the station for an attendant. I don't see anyone, so I put the nozzle into the tank and begin pumping the gas.

"Y'all must be looking for Silas Harrow." The voice takes me by surprise, and I spin around to be face to face with an old man. He has on a pair of overalls and a blue trucker cap. He spits tobacco juice onto the stained pavement. "We don't see many kids around here that we don't know. Usually, when we do, it turns out they're looking for him."

"Okay," I say. "You got me."

"Over yonder." The man points across the parking lot. "On the other side of those pines is an old farm owned by a man named Johnson. His boy was the last one to spot him."

"How long ago was it?" I ask.

The man surprises me by looking at the watch. "Couldn't of been more than half an hour ago."

The gas pump turns off, indicating the

car's tank is full. "Well, thank you, sir." I put the nozzle back on the pump. "Let me run in here and pay, and I'll be out of your way."

"You can pay me," he says. "I'm the only one here."

I reach into my back pocket, pull out my wallet, and hand him a twenty. "Thank you," I tell him. "Do you happen to know the name of the guy who saw him?"

The man laughs. "Kid, I know the name of everybody around here. That's just the way it is. It was Trevor Henderson, if you've got to know."

I swing open the car door and sit down behind the wheel. Just as I am about to pull the door closed, the man asks me something else. "Why do you want to know anyway?"

Not wanting to get into the whole thing about how I'm here looking for Dad, I say, "I have my reasons. Have a good day." And I close the door.

When I'm pulling out of the parking lot, I glance in the rearview mirror. The man is standing there, watching us.

"We're getting close," I tell Kristen.

From the gas station, I follow the man's vague lead and turn down the narrow road on the left. It is a straight shot without any intersecting roads, and I keep going.

It doesn't take long for us to reach the farm. Now it is completely dark, and the car's headlights illuminate what's in front of us. The farm is overgrown and looks like it hasn't been worked in years. A rusty barbed wire fence runs alongside the property, and I can see a pair of worn tire tracks that run perpendicular to the fence and ditch bank. I turn the car onto the dirt road.

"Are you sure we should be doing this?" Kristen asks. "What if this is private property? We could get shot."

"I'm not sure we should be doing *any* of this." I tell her. "But it's not private property. There was a stop sign back there. This is a public road."

The car bumps over the ruts in the red dirt, and we make a sharp turn around an old a cow barn. There's the glow of red brake lights in front of us. Kristen sees them too. "Mackenzie," she says and puts her hand on mine. "There are people out here. We need to turn around."

"What if it's Dad?" I ask. "What if *he's* out here?"

Now it is clear that there are actually several trucks parked in front of us. The largest truck is still running and is blocking the road. If something happens, it's going to be difficult to turn around.

"What if it's *not* him?" Kristin fires back. "Who knows what these people are up to."

There is a loose circle of people at the edge of the field, and everyone in the group turns to look at us.

I pull up as close as I can to the congregation and put the car in park. My eyes scan the crowd, searching for Dad. Without counting, I imagine there are about a dozen people in all. It is a mixture of men and women, young and old. But none of them are who I'm looking for. I reach for the door handle.

"You're not going out there," Kristen tells me. "This is a bad idea, Mackenzie."

I stare into her eyes. "I have to. They might know where he is. I'll be okay. Lock the car while I'm gone." I open the door and step out of the car.

There is a middle-aged woman with frizzy blonde hair behind the wheel of the largest truck. I notice a tacky ceramic blue jay stuck to the truck's dash.

I step through the tall field grass until I am standing next to the group. The ground is covered with white and purple flowers. The scene is pretty, but, being in such close proximity to the barn, it smells like cow shit. A man steps forward. Judging by his posture and features, he seems to be in his mid-twenties. His head is shaved, and he is wearing an old Members Only jacket. His hands are shoved deep in the front pockets of his baggy jeans. Once he is closer, I notice a silver loop through his left eyebrow.

"I'm looking for my Dad," I tell him. "I thought he might be out here."

"Why do you think he might be *here*?" The guy asks me.

I cross my arms tight across my chest. "Well, he's into this kind of stuff…"

"What kind of stuff do you think this is?" He cuts me off.

My eyes dart past the dude's right shoulder, and I see that the rest of the crowd is staring at us.

"Silas Harrow," I tell him. "I thought…"

"Are you a believer?"

The question takes me by surprise. I don't know how to answer. Or *what* I'm answering *to*.

He puts his hand on my shoulder. "It's a yes or no question, kid. You either believe or you don't," he says. "I'm going to ask you one more time…"

I know what the right answer is. "Yes," I

tell him

We stay that way for a moment. With his hand on my shoulder, he is looking me in the eyes. Can he tell that I'm lying?

He pats my shoulder and then finally takes his hand off me. "As you can imagine, we get a lot of naysayers around here. We see a lot of people out here just looking to take selfies. If you can promise me that you and your girl aren't here for shits and giggles, I can let you talk to Trevor."

Trevor. Trevor Henderson, I remember. He is the one that the man at the gas station mentioned, the one that supposedly spotted Silas earlier tonight. Surely Dad has talked to him. If anybody knows where Dad might be, Trevor is my best shot.

I let it sink in that this sketchy dude has seen Kristen in the car. It disturbs me to realize that he knows she's here.

"I promise," I say.

He nods and then puts his fingers in his mouth and whistles. "Hey, send Trevor over here," he yells to the group. The crowd parts and a young man steps forward. He is tall and lanky. His greasy blonde hair is hanging down in front of his face. He walks up to us and stands right in front of me.

"My buddy here's looking for his Dad," the first guy tells Trevor.

"There was an older man out here a little bit ago," Trevor says. "He's gone now, but, before he left, he said something about going to his parents' place."

So Dad *was* here. He's already left the field, but he's still in Trenton.

"Thank you," I tell both of them. I turn around and can feel them staring at me as I walk away.

CHAPTER NINE

DAD'S CHILDHOOD HOME is a dilapidated structure. The two-story farmhouse is made of weathered board and tin. Several of the windows are busted out, and sheets of plastic have been tacked to the inside of the window frames. In some places, the plastic is flapping in the increasing nighttime breeze.

The yard is overgrown with weeds and wildflowers. A tire swing hangs from a drooping branch of a walnut tree. The tree reminds me of a story Dad told me one time.   Growing up, the family didn't have a lot of money, and he and his sister had to make do with what was already there. With their imagination, Dad and Sally were able to turn the walnut tree into hours worth of good fun—Dad used one of the limbs and the walnuts to play baseball while Sally cheered him on with a leafy branch that she used as a pompom.

Aside from a dim streetlight behind the house, the lot is dark. No one has lived here for several years. Dad still owns the house, but he's been renting it out ever since he moved to the island. From what I remember, the last renters were trouble-makers, and Dad had to have them evicted.

As we approach the abandoned lot, I spot Dad's truck parked behind the house.

"Why would he come back *here*?" Kristen asks.

"Beats the heck out of me," I tell her. "I don't think the place even has power."

I pull the car into the driveway and pass an orange and black *No Trespassing* sign that is nailed to a large oak tree.

Several yards down the gravel drive, the car bounces, and I hear a loud exclamation of air. The vehicle drops and skids to a halt. I hear a thump of rubber and know we have a flat.

I swing open my door and lean my head out. The left-side rim is on the ground. I look back to see what we might have hit and spot several broken glass bottles.

My eyes dart to Dad's truck at the back of the house. "We just go in the house, find Dad, and he'll be able to help us."

After putting the car in park, we get out. As we're walking away, I turn around and notice that *both* of the front tires are flat.

We are making our way across the yard, closer to the sagging front porch, when my foot gets tangled in something on the ground. Whatever it is nearly causes me to trip, but I manage to catch myself before I fall on my ass. I kick my foot away from what I now see is a pile of wadded plastic. It's one of those tacky holiday yard inflatables. Actually, there are several of them on the ground around us. I notice several bright colors—green, purple, and orange.

One of the inflatables near Kristen is moving. Rustling. Something must be under it, I realize. "Kristen..." I start to tell her to step back. It could be a rabid coon or some other wild animal.

I pull out my phone and turn on the flashlight app. A moment later, *all* of the inflatables are moving. I swing my phone around, and the light casts a glow over everything. Kristen steps closer to me and puts her hand on my back.

All of a sudden, the inflatables shoot up in a loud, audible whoosh. There are three of them in all, and the figures are looming over us. I immediately recognize the holiday they represent—Halloween. It's eerie to have the spooky décor around us in the middle of April.

"I thought you said the power is out."

"I figured it would be," I tell her and look toward the house. Now all of the interior lights are on. I switch off the phone's flashlight app and put the phone in my front pocket.

Kristen and I walk past the Halloween

decorations and up the creaky front steps. The floorboards of the porch feel like they could easily give way under our weight. The front door is unlocked, and we go inside. "Dad?" I call out. My voice echoes off the bare walls.

I go up the stairs, and Kristen follows close behind.

On the second floor, there is a long hallway with doors on each side. The door at the end of the hall is backlit. It is Dad's old room.

We reach the end of the walkway, and I push the door open.

Right away, I notice something on the floor in the center of the otherwise bare room. A book. I walk over to it and kneel down. It is an old, clothbound copy of *The Island of Dr. Moreau*. I pick up the book and tuck it into the waistband of my jeans.

After checking the other rooms, it's obvious that Dad's not up here, and we hurry back down the steps. When we round the corner, there's a shadow that moves past the plastic that's covering one of the windows. The figure stands still on the other side.

"Dad?" My voice cracks. "Is that you?"

The silhouette is tall and thin. The fingers look long and twisted. The thought crosses my mind that Dad and all of those weirdoes at the cow pasture are right. Maybe Silas Harrow *is* real.

The figure steps away from the window, and Kristen and I start moving toward the front door. When we round the corner, the door is opening. Whoever, *whatever* it is, is coming inside.

I grab Kristen's hand, and we run in the opposite direction. I hear the figure moving behind us—in the house—but I don't pause to see how close it's getting.

The first room we come to is a small bathroom. I lead Kristen inside and drop her hand. I start to close the door, but the floor is uneven, and I can hear the scrape of wood. The door is stuck. There is a thud on the other side, and I feel the resistance of it being pushed back.

Kristen unlatches the window and pulls it up. The old counterweights rattle inside the wall. "It won't go any further," she says.

I slam my body weight into the door, but it still won't budge. I look up and notice that it's not just the uneven floor that is causing the problem. A metal towel rack is hooked over the top of the door. There is no way to get the door closed and locked. "Break it," I say.

A second later, there's the sound of shattering glass. I step away from the door, and

Kristen is climbing out the window. I move backward, keeping my eye on the intruder until it is my turn to go. A hand reaches through the gap between the door and its frame. One by one, the fingers curl around the edge. But it's only fingers, I realize. Actual human fingers. The nails are painted pink, and I hear each of them click against the solid oak. The hand rattles and pushes on the door until it bangs against the vanity.

I'm at the window now, climbing through. The broken glass cuts into my hands and arms. The figure in the doorway steps forward. It is not Silas Harrow. It is a woman with frizzy blonde hair.

"Mackenzie," she says. "Wait. I need to talk to you."

From the window, I drop several feet to the ground, and the woman steps up to the open space. She is wearing a pink tank top and a pair of denim cut offs. I can smell the stale cigarette smoke coming off her. If she's there to do something bad, there's no way she'd be able to get to us fast enough. So I wait to hear her out.

"My name is Loretta," she says. "I know your daddy. He's out in the truck."

I turn my head to look and see a pickup truck with large tires. In the moonlight, the truck looks dark blue. From the distance, I can't tell if the slumped-over figure inside the cab really is Dad or not.

"Y'all wait right there," Loretta says.

A minute later, Loretta exits the house through the front door and then motions for us to join her next to the front porch.

"I run The Jukebox," she tells us, and we start walking with her toward the truck. "Your daddy came in this afternoon and, after a few drinks, started talking all kinds of nonsense about Silas Harrow. When he left, this is where he went. I came by the house to check on him and found him inside. I got him in the truck and was just about to leave when I spotted y'all."

Once we are standing beside Loretta's truck, I realize that she is telling the truth. It *is* Dad in there. He lifts his head and looks at us, smiles, and drops his head back down. I can tell he's drunk.

Loretta opens the door, and Kristen and I climb into the back seat. I notice the ceramic bluebird on the dash and realize that it is the same truck that I saw in the field earlier.

"I'll take you to the motel over in Edgefield. He just needs to sleep it off, and he'll be fine." Loretta turns the key in the ignition. "My son Justin can fix your tires in the morning.

He owns a shop. People around town say he's the best mechanic there is."

We sit in silence until after we're on the road, and Loretta starts talking again. "I grew up with your daddy and Sally." She pauses at the mention of my aunt. Other than Dad and my grandparents, I'd never met anybody that knew her. Sally died when she was ten years old.

Loretta continues. "In fact, I lived right down the road from them. Your daddy and I are the same age. We were a thing one time." Her face turns red at the mention of their romance. "Anyway, we started this little monster hunting club with some of the other kids around town. We had a lot of fun back then."

It only takes us a few minutes to get to the motel. It is a sketchy-looking structure that stands alone on the dark road.

Loretta steers the truck into the parking lot, and the tires bounce over the deep potholes in the asphalt.

"Sorry about the look of the place," she tells us. "But Jim and Kathy are real nice people. They keep it clean on the inside." She parks and hops down out of the cab. "Let me go get y'all checked in, and I'll be right back." She closes the door and walks across the parking lot to the motel's office.

"We don't know this woman." Kristen speaks quietly. "What if she's leading us into some kind of trap? She could kill all three of us, and nobody would ever know."

There is only one other car in the parking lot. The motel is surrounded on all four sides by acres of dense pine trees. It *does* look like a place where a body could be dumped and not found for years.

"We won't let her in," I tell her. "We'll get Dad inside the room and then send Loretta on her way."

"She could have a key," Kristen points out the obvious.

I glance up, and Loretta is already walking back toward the truck. "Come on," I say and open the door. We get out, and I open Dad's door. He mumbles something that I can't understand, and I help him to his feet. I throw my arm around his shoulders to keep him steady. Now, Loretta is standing in front of us.

"I think we can get it from here," I say. "Thanks for all your help."

Loretta nods and hands me the motel keys. She starts to walk away, but then she stops and turns around. "I believe your daddy's right, by the way. It wasn't just the game that killed that boy. Something else is going on."

"Something with Silas Harrow, you mean?"

Loretta shakes her head. "If he's real or not, it doesn't matter. Made up stories can cause just as much trouble as real ones. It takes some people a long time to get over things, and some people never do. Hold on a second. Let me give you my number."

She goes to her truck and returns with a small, folded piece of paper that I slip into my back pocket. After Loretta leaves, I call Mom and let her know that I found Dad and that the three of us will be spending the night in Trenton.

CHAPTER TEN

I CAN'T SLEEP. I'm sitting upright on one of the motel's two double beds. Kristen is lying next to me, asleep, and Dad is snoring in the other bed. The TV is on in front of us, but the volume is set so low that the dialogue is undecipherable. This is not how I'd imagined my first time spending a night in a motel with a girl would go.

Since being here overnight was not planned, neither of us have a change of clothes or essential toiletries. Kristen went to the motel office where she picked up complimentary toothbrushes and toothpaste from the attendant. With the available soap and shampoo, both of us were able to take showers before lying down and trying to get some sleep, wearing the same clothes we've had on all day.

Some of Loretta's last words from earlier are haunting me — *"It wasn't just the game that killed that boy. Something else is going on."* I still can't wrap my head around the possibility of David's death being caused by Silas Harrow, and if David dying wasn't an accident, there are two other possibilities — suicide or murder.

Trying to get my mind off the subject, I turn on the reading lamp and pick up the copy of *The Island of Doctor Moreau* that I found in

Dad's old bedroom.

I run my fingers over the front cover and then open the book. The inside page is scribbled with pencil marks. I flip through the pages. There is a library card holder on the inside of the back cover. I pull the card out of the pocket and scan through the list of students who've checked the book out.

Dad's name is printed several times, but it is the last name on the card that startles me. I sit up straight. *Sally Walker*. Dad's sister. My eyes dart to the right side of the card to where the due dates have been stamped. Sally checked the book out in 1996.

But that can't be right, I think.

I close the book and nudge Kristen. I talk low so I don't wake Dad. "Kristen, get up."

She stirs, and her eyes open. "What time is it?"

I'm already standing. "A little after midnight," I tell her.

"What's going on?" She sits up on the edge of the bed. "Is everything okay?"

"Come outside. There's something I need to show you."

Kristen follows me across the room. I slide the back door open as quietly as I can. The vertical blinds clatter with the movement, and the sound causes me to glance at Dad again. I'm relieved to see he's still sleeping.

We step onto the back porch, and I shut the door. The porch is a narrow concrete slab with a wobbly wooden rail that I lean my butt against. There's a stretch of dark woods across from us. I flip to the back of the book. "Look at this," I pull out the card and pass it to her. "According to this, Sally was the last person to borrow it."

"Yeah," she says. "And she never returned it." She pulls her arms tight across her abdomen and yawns. "Shame on her. 1996. Imagine the late fee that she must have by now."

I shake my head. "I've always been told that Sally died when Dad was eleven. This checkout is from '96. Dad would have been eighteen."

Kristen's eyes widen, and she hands the card back to me.

"He's been lying about this all along," I tell her, and it hurts to admit the fact about my own father.

After we go back inside, I stretch out on the bed with my back toward Kristen so that I'm facing Dad. It doesn't take long for Kristen to fall asleep, but it's not that easy for me. David Fiske, Silas Harrow, and Dad's lie are all wrapping themselves around each other in my brain.

Eventually I doze off into a fitful sleep. When I wake, I'm surprised to see daylight slipping through the blinds. The next thing I notice is that Kristen's arm is thrown over me, and her hand is resting low on my belly. I close my eyes to take in this moment, savoring it.

But the thrill doesn't last long. When I open my eyes again, I notice that the other bed is empty. Dad is not here.

I don't want to move, but I know I have to. I ease myself out from under Kristen's arm. As I'm sitting up, I feel her shift behind me. I turn around and see that she's already propped herself up on her elbow.

"Dad's gone again." I stand from the bed, walk across the room, and swing the door open. The morning sunlight is blinding. I squint my eyes and see Loretta walking toward me.

"I was going to let y'all sleep a little bit longer," she says. "Checkout's not till eleven."

"What's going on?" I ask. "Where's Dad?"

Loretta uses her thumb to point over her shoulder. I see Dad in the cab of the truck, drinking coffee from a throwaway cup. Now Kristen is standing beside me in the doorway.

"Justin's already towed the car," Loretta

says. "I was fixing to take your daddy back to the house for his truck. How about I drive you to the next town over. You can get a bite to eat, and your daddy can meet you there. Justin's shop will be right around the corner."

I haven't eaten since the drive-thru yesterday afternoon, and the thought of a hot breakfast sounds amazing. Plus, now that I know Dad is safe, I feel like I can finally sit down and enjoy a proper meal.

Kristin and I go back into the room and put on our shoes. Then we climb into the backseat of Loretta's truck, and Dad turns his head to look at us. I introduce him and Kristen to one another, and I'm surprised that Dad doesn't ask questions.

The next town is only a mile or so away, and Loretta drops me and Kristen off on the square. When I get out of the truck, I take a quick second to look around. There's a brick courthouse, a library, and several businesses.

"There's a few places you can get a bite to eat," Loretta tells us. "Just pick one. You can't go wrong. Justin's shop is right over there."

The auto shop sits cattycorner to the library. I notice the rental car is already up on a jack.

After Loretta drives away with Dad,

Kristen and I choose a little mom-and-pop diner. Kristin opens the door, and a cowbell rings. I follow her inside. A woman from behind the counter looks up at us. "Y'all can sit wherever you want."

Kristin picks a table by the window where two menus are already waiting. A minute later, the waiter comes over and takes our order.

It doesn't take long to get the food, and we're just finishing our breakfast when I see Dad's truck pull into one of the parking spaces out front. He comes inside and joins us at the table where he orders scrambled eggs, bacon, and coffee.

After our meal, Dad takes us over to the auto shop where the rental car is now off the jack and is parked out front. I notice that both of the front tires are new. I go inside with Dad. Loretta's son, Justin, is behind the counter. I immediately recognize him as the same guy with the eyebrow ring from the field the night before.

After Dad pays and we return to our vehicles, I wait until Dad has driven away before I exit the parking lot. The mystery of what I saw in the back of the library book—the date that Aunt Sally checked out the book versus her supposed date of death—is still fresh in my mind, and I want to investigate before I leave town.

After driving around the area, I am able to find the cemetery where Aunt Sally's grave is located. The small cemetery sits behind an old white church that looks exactly like I remember. I park the car in the gravel parking in front of the church.

The cemetery is enclosed by a wrought iron fence, and the tombstones are old and weathered. Kristen and I follow the path that leads all the way to the back corner. When we get to the grave, I look down and read the inscription on the tombstone. *Sally—Our Beloved Daughter*. There is also a smaller granite marker at the foot of the grave, a marker that likely has the last name of the deceased. The inscription says *Johnson*. This is some Sally Johnson buried here, *not* my Aunt.

"It's not her," I say. "That's not his sister that's buried out here."

Once we get back to the car, I reach into my back pocket and pull out the piece of paper that Loretta gave me. I unfold it and notice that the sheet of stationary has a sketched bluebird at the top. I dial the number, and Loretta answers after the first ring.

"What do you know about Dad's sister?" I cut right to the chase.

"We were friends," Loretta tells me. "But...after the accident...she just disappeared."

"Accident?"

"The prank, Mackenzie. You don't know?"

"No. I have no idea what you're talking about."

"Twenty years ago, Sally and one of our friends were going to stage a Silas Harrow hanging, and the guy died. A lot of people blamed Sally for the whole thing, and I haven't seen or heard from her since." She takes a deep breath. "Your daddy thinks the guy's death on the island is connected to all of that."

After I get off the phone with Loretta, I tell Kristen everything I just learned. "The fact of the matter is that someone died, and Sally disappeared. Dad has been lying about it my whole life. Before he came here, he said he thinks that David's death has something to do with Silas Harrow. With what Loretta just told me about Sally and the prank... What if Dad is right? What if everything is connected?"

"Do you think we should tell somebody?" Kristen asks.

I take a second to let everything start to sink in. Obviously, there's more to the story. I know what people would think if we say something—with the fact that Dad has been lying about his sister's death for so long, what else could he be hiding? They would immediately think he is up to something. Dad might be a flake, but I can't throw him under the bus for no reason. "How about this," I say. "We go to the cops if we find anything on the island that even remotely links David's death to all of this."

CHAPTER ELEVEN

DURING THE BOATRIDE back to the resort, I get the sense that the water that separates us from the mainland isn't as wide as I've always thought; the past and the present, this world and that, are closer than I believed. Even so, it is the future that I'm worried about.

Once we're back on the island, I realize what we need to do. In order to have a better idea of what happened to David, we need to know more about him. So, for the second time in two days, I snoop on his social media.

The first three images are all selfies. David is wearing the same shirt in each one, and I realize that they were all taken on the same night—the night he died. I notice that he has a tattoo on his right bicep. The tattoo is that of a wagon wheel.

I begin to scroll faster through the posts. It is the usual, exactly what I'd expect to see—fraternity brothers, girls, beer, food, and work-out pics. Based on everything I see, David seemed to be a popular, well-liked guy. Then, abruptly, I reach the end. I click on the first post he did under the account. It is a picture of what I assume is the green space on his college campus. The date is from September of last year.

The fact that he didn't start posting until September strikes me as kind of strange. To me, it seems like a popular, good looking guy like David would be all over social media and have tons of friends and followers.

Frustrated, I pull up the internet browser on my phone. I type his name into the search box.

I click on the *Images* tab. After I scroll through pictures of other people with the same name, I finally see one that catches my eye, and I click on it. It is a picture of three geeky-looking guys, each with long, shaggy hair. They are all wearing black t-shirts that have superhero images printed on the front. The picture was taken at some sort of convention.

The date of the picture is from April of last year, only five months before David started the personal page. I enlarge the picture and look closer at the guy in the middle. He is flabby and out of shape, but it is undeniably the same David Fiske. The same smile. The same eyes. The same tattoo of the wagon wheel is peeking out from under his t-shirt sleeve.

It doesn't make any sense. The group of guys I'm looking at are not the type to join a fraternity. Instead, they are the kind that were likely bullied when they were younger and then stayed far away from the popular crowd. I know their type—I'm one of them.

So how and why, in such a short period of time, did David go from what I'm seeing here to the person that arrived on the island a few days earlier? In five months, he completely changed. Obviously he'd been hitting the gym over that summer, but it had to be more to it than that.

I go back to the search bar and type in *Wagon Wheel*. I scroll through the links until I find a page on symbolism. *The wheel is a symbol of power*, it says, solidifying the idea in my mind that fraternities are weird.

The more I try to wrap my brain around all of this and what it means to David's death, if anything, the more confused I get.

Kristen and I decide to go to The Mandevilla shortly after dark. There are a few people splashing around in the pool, but it is nothing like it was a couple of nights earlier. Caleb is sitting on the diving board. Again, he is wearing the beer-case cowboy hat.

We take the elevator up to the fifth floor. The hallway is vacant. Since most of the fraternity left, no one else has checked in. Once we are standing in front of the room, I pull out the master key that I'd swiped from Mom's office.

The inside of the room is clean. The bed is made. The shelf that the three guys were using for the choking game is back on the wall. There is no sign that someone died in here just two nights earlier.

Searching for something that would link David to Silas Harrow, we look in all of the drawers, under the bed, behind the furniture, *everywhere*, but we can't find anything.

I pull out my phone and go to David's social media again. I'm hoping that being in the room where it happened, maybe I can get a better idea of the events that led up to his death by studying the selfies from earlier that night.

On one of the pictures, David is holding a beer toward the camera, and there is a crowd of college students behind him. There is one among the crowd that stands out from all the rest. She is wearing a blue button down shirt, and her arms are crossed tight over her chest. I touch the screen and zoom in closer. It is Brockley.

So—Brockley was in the room with David just an hour prior to his death. In the photo, she is glaring at him, obviously pissed about something. I wonder if David knew she was even there.

"Look at this," I tell Kristen and hand her the phone. Her mouth drops open.

I remember the night that I found Brockley crying in the dunes. It couldn't have been long after David posted this.

"I think we might be looking in the wrong room. If Brockley knew David, maybe she can tell us something."

THE NEXT DAY, Kristen and I make a loop around the gardens, expecting to find Brockley, but each of the gardens is empty. On the day that I'd spotted Brockley studying the corpse flower, a bicycle was leaning against the fence. That means she'd rented a bike, and her name and room number would be on the paperwork.

"I know how to find out where she's staying," I say.

Once we get to The Bike Shed, I pull open the top drawer of the filing cabinet and flip through the folders until I find the one that I'm looking for. I pull the folder, lay it flat on the countertop, and flip through the papers until I find the one with her name on it.

"Room 315, Oleander." I say out loud. "This is it," I tell Kristen. I fold the paper in half and slip it into my back pocket.

Hotel Oleander is lazy this early in the morning. Kristin and I walk up to the front of the building, and I notice that the ground around the shrubbery is broken like some sort of plant is trying to push its way to the surface. Kristen tells me that she's going to wait outside, and I don't blame her.

Alone, I walk down the hallway until I'm standing in front of the room that I came for. I knock on the door. There is no answer, and I knock again, louder this time. Now I hear the sound of the chain and deadbolt from the other side. The door swings open. It is not Brockley. This is a girl with long brown hair that's pulled back in a ponytail. I vaguely recognize her, but I can't figure out why or from where.

"What?" The girl asks. Her eyes are heavy. I can tell she's just waking up, and I imagine that she has been out partying all night. Then I know where I know her from. She is the girl that was puking in the grass outside of The Mandevilla on the night of the pool party.

"Is Brockley around?" I ask her.

The girl rolls her eyes. "Brockley didn't even sleep here last night," she tells me. "I haven't seen her in two days."

My eyes dart over the girl's shoulder, and I scan the room. The space is cluttered with clothes. On the back counter there's a scattering of girly things—makeup, a hairdryer, and bath stuff. But there is something else about the room that grabs my attention.

A small potted plant is on the nightstand that is furthest away from the door. The plant's stems are long, but the leaves are droopy. It needs water.

"Who's plant is that?" I ask.

The girl rolls her eyes and laughs. "Not mine," she says. "Brockley takes that stupid thing with her everywhere she goes."

I know something isn't right. Aside from the fact that Brockley is strange enough to take the plant with her on spring break, if the plant really is that important to her, she wouldn't leave it to wither and die in the hotel room.

"I'm kind of worried about her to tell you the truth," the girl says. "Hooking up with a guy who winds up dead later the same night could screw with your head, you know?"

The statement stops me cold. "You mean her and David…"

"Yep. I tried to tell her it was a mistake."

So David was the reason that Brockley was crying outside of The Mandevilla on the night of the party. At least *one* of the reasons, I remind myself. Brockley seems like the type that could have a lot going on.

"Afterwards, she said he gave her his

phone number, but it was a fake," the girl continues. "Typical frat boy crap." She rolls her eyes.

I remember that Brockley had a piece of paper with her that night in the dunes. After I sat down, she crumpled the paper and tossed it into the grass. If it was David that she was crying over, the piece of paper might be the only thing we have that connects her to him. It hasn't rained in the past few days, and the tide hasn't been coming in too high. Unless a bird or hermit crab has carried the paper away, it might still be there.

"Well, just tell her Mackenzie came by," I say.

"Yeah. Okay. Whatever." She slams the door in my face.

"We need to go back to The Mandevilla," I tell Kristen once I meet up with her outside. I tell her about the paper that David gave Brockley and that I think it might still be there.

Once we get to the other hotel, we step into the dunes. I look around and place myself in the proximity of where I was sitting when I was talking to Brockley that night. Then I spot the wadded note among the tall reeds. I pick up the paper and flatten it out against the palm of my hand. The ink is fading, but the number is still decipherable. There are no dashes or anything to indicate that it is a phone number.

"If it's not a phone number, what is it?" Kristin asks. "If David wanted her gone, maybe he just wrote down some kind of gibberish and handed it to her."

It's a horrible thing to think, but I know she's right. Guys like David can be cruel. Not *all* of them, but it's too common.

If what we are thinking is right—that the paper connects Brockley to David—what could the number be that would link both of them to Dad and the legend of Silas Harrow? What is the one thing that would bring all of this together?

Then, I know. "It could be a code."

WHEN I WENT into the lab with Vinyl when I was thirteen years old, I used a key card. Technology has moved at a rapid pace in the past four years. The old keycard entry system has been replaced by a touch screen lock-pad that requires a password.

Now, Kristen and I are standing in front of the door. It is night. I can hear the distant sound of waves crashing on the shore and the occasional hoop and holler of spring break partiers.

I take a look around to make sure that nobody is nearby. The coast is clear. I pull the paper out of my pocket and gather my thoughts.

If the code doesn't unlock the door, I have been way off course. In that case, maybe Dad or Silas Harrow has nothing at all to do with David's death.

But if the code works—that means David had access to Dad's top secret lab, and it would directly connect Dad to a dead frat boy.

I take a deep breath. "Here goes nothing," I tell Kristen and put the numbers into the keypad.

After I hit the final digit, there is a long pause where nothing happens. I take a deep sigh of relief, and then, just as I'm about to turn away, I hear it.

The unmistakable sound of the lock undoing.

It is the code to the door.

CHAPTER TWELVE

THESE ARE THE facts—David had the code to Dad's laboratory in his possession, and he gave the number to Brockley. Now David is dead, and Brockley is missing.

"We've got to go to the police," Kristen says. "Now, Mackenzie."

She starts to turn away, and I grab her arm. "Kristen, wait..."

She spins around so that she is facing me again. "What other proof do you need?" She asks. "Both of the people that we know for sure had their hands on that piece of paper are gone—one of them is dead—and now you're the one holding it."

Just two days ago, I wanted more than anything for Dad to realize that he was only chasing a fairytale when he ran off to Trenton, but now I desperately want the legend of Silas Harrow to be real. That strange possibility is infinitely better than the alternative.

The alarm sounds from inside the laboratory. Out of the corner of my eye, I notice the light on the side of the house come on. I look and see a shadow moving around on the other side of the kitchen windows. A second later, the backdoor opens, and Dad is standing on the screened-in porch. He has a flashlight in his hand.

How could we have been so stupid to not think about the alarm in the lab?

My eyes dart around the area looking for somewhere to hide. There is nowhere to go that would put us out of Dad's sight quick enough. So I grab Kristen's hand, and the two of us run through the laboratory door. As soon as we are in the hallway, I let her hand go, turn around, and pull the door closed behind us.

The steady, rhythmic beep of the alarm continues. The sound is loud and makes the scenario even more tense. The overhead lights are off, but there is a steady, bright flash that goes along with the beeping of the alarm.

Dad will be swinging the main door open any second now, and, when he does, we need to be out of sight.

"This way," I tell Kristen and grab her hand again. Together, we run down the hall toward the set of double doors that are waiting at the opposite end. Four years earlier, Vinyl and I approached those same doors with a sense of curiosity. Now, the doors serve as a barrier. They separate us from a place of attainable safety and the possible danger of what is behind us—my father. The uncertainty of both scenarios sets me on edge.

I shove the right-side door open, and, on the other side, there is nothing but darkness. Kristen and I step in, and I hear the door swing shut behind us. It is a relief that there is no flashing light in here, but I can still hear the rhythmic beep of the alarm. The sound is muffled now, but it is there, nonetheless.

Kristen pulls out her phone and flips on the flashlight app. She holds the phone up and shines the light around the space. With the light, I am able to catch glimpses of tall, looming plants.

Abruptly, the alarm stops, and from behind us comes the heavy sound of the main door closing. I know what all of this means. Dad is in the building.

Kristen turns off the light, and we move to the far back corner where we crouch down low behind one of the largest plants. The enormous terra-cotta pot is cracked all the way up the side, and the plant's roots are exposed and stretched across the floor.

In a dramatic move, Dad pushes both of the doors open simultaneously and flips on the overhead light. From where I am behind the plant, my pulse is thrumming as I peek around the pot and watch Dad survey what is in front of him. Finally, he turns around and goes back through the swinging doors. He didn't see us, I realize, and I can finally feel my heart-rate begin to ease.

We stand up and step quietly. Something moves behind us. It sounds like something being dragged. Then, one of the huge ceramic planters slides several inches across the concrete. I realize that whatever we are hearing just nudged and moved one of the largest plants in the room.

Kristen still has her phone out, and she flips on the flashlight app again. She holds the phone up and jerks the light from the left to the right, looking for whatever it is that is in the room with us.

Then, in the shadowy area between the plants, something unfurls from the darkness. Kristen spins the light around so that it lands on the nightmarish thing that is in front of us—a moving tendril that is as big as my arm, uncurling, reaching toward us. I hear Kristen gasp, and the two of us turn around and run.

I stop at the swinging doors. Through the narrow crack where the two doors meet, I see Dad standing at the opposite end of the hallway. He is putting the last digits into the alarm's keypad. When he steps away, there is a steady beep and a flashing red light from the box on the wall. It is the countdown to the alarm being reset. There is only forty-five seconds to get out of the lab without triggering the alarm. Dad pushes the door open, steps outside, and lets the door slam shut behind him.

I glance back at the monstrous thing that is behind us and grab Kristen's hand once again. "Let's go," I tell her.

We shove our way through the double doors and run down the hall. When we get to the end, I drop Kristen's hand and lean toward the peephole that is on the exit door. What I see is a fisheye view of the yard and everything that stands beyond. There is a narrow expanse of open grass, and the beginning of the woods is not far behind. I don't see Dad out there. I wait, giving him more time to get back inside the house.

The beeping from the alarm gets faster. I know that it is on its final countdown. We have to get out now, or we will set the alarm off again. I'm not sure where Dad is on the other side, but I push the door open anyway. Kristen runs out first, and I close the door as quietly as I can behind us.

Outside, I bend over with my hands on my knees, and I'm finally able to catch my breath. When I stand up straight, my eyes dart around the yard, looking for Dad. He is walking up the porch steps.

Dad hadn't heard the door, I realize. And he hadn't seen us either. We are in the clear. He pulls the screen door open and is about to go inside when...

He turns around.

CHAPTER THIRTEEN

DAD SHINES THE flashlight in our direction. The light blinds me, and I'm sure I look like a deer caught in headlights.

He steps down from the porch and begins walking to where we're standing. My heart is hammering in my chest. The laboratory is off limits, and I know that I'm going to be in trouble for going in. Plus, there's the added idea of Dad being up to something *really* bad that continues to creep around in my mind.

There's nowhere to go, and Kristen and I stand still. A second later, Dad is right in front of us. "What are you doing out here?" He is staring at me.

For some reason, I glance at his hands. I imagine them wrapped tight around David's neck, strangling him. Was David killed for the same thing that Kristen and I just did—for going into the lab?

"Where did you get the code?" Dad asks matter-of-factly.

I don't answer. I don't know *how*. I know that if I tell him the truth—that we found it where Brockley left it in the dunes during the night of the frat party—he would know that I know. Instead of coming up with an excuse, I just shake my head.

"Take her back to the campsite," Dad nods his head toward Kristen and then locks eyes with me. "You and I will talk about this later." He turns around and starts to make his way back to the house.

I walk Kristen to where the golf cart is parked underneath the carport. After we sit down, I turn the key in the ignition and the motor flips over. A few seconds later, we are on the dirt road that will lead us to the beach.

"What the heck *was* that thing?" Kristen asks. I know that she is talking about the reaching plant tendril we saw in the lab. "It was like something from a horror movie."

As I drive, I tell her about the rampantly growing vines on the cell tower and how, after I cut them off, they came back overnight. "It was kind of like that," I say, "but the one in the lab was worse. Bigger."

"Do you think it might be one of your Dad's experiments?"

"It's crossed my mind," I admit, "but, honestly, I don't know what to think about *any* of this. David, Brockley, Silas, the experiments, my aunt. None of it makes any sense, and, no matter what, I can't seem to connect the dots."

We ride in silence for several yards.

Spanish Moss hangs from the old oaks that stand on each side of the road. The moon is full, but the canopy of thick tree cover barely lets any of the moonlight through. Under other, normal circumstances, the scene could be considered romantic.

"What are you going to tell your Dad?" Kristen asks. "The reason we went in there?"

My thoughts ramble with different answers to what I know will be an unavoidable question when I get back home, and I eventually settle on what I'm going to say. "I'll tell him that we snuck in so we could make out." As soon as I say it, I feel my face turning red, and I don't look at Kristen. I realize how stupid the statement was. Why would we go in there when we have the entire island? Kristen's silence sets me on edge.

We emerge from the trees, and I make a sharp turn onto a sandy stretch of beach where I pull to a stop but leave the golf cart running.

From where we're sitting, the breeze coming off the ocean is cool. I can hear the waves crashing against the shore, and there's a clear view of a small party at the campsite. Orange embers from a bonfire float into the sky where they mingle with the stars. Suddenly, there's the thump of heavy bass from nearby speakers, and I notice a girl stand up and begin booty dancing in sync with the rap music. She's wearing a hula skirt and coconut bra.

"Is that Tina?" Kristen laughs and leans forward to get a better look.

From here, the red hair is a dead giveaway. "Yeah, I think it is."

Kristen laughs out loud, covers her mouth with her hand, and flings herself back against the seat.

With her laughter, it's a happy moment that almost takes my mind away from everything else that is going on. It hurts me to think about how things could be between me and Kristen if all of this other stuff hadn't gotten in the way. More than ever, I have the feeling that if I had a normal life things would be different. Better.

"You shouldn't be involved in any of this," I tell her. "It's spring break. You should be out there, having fun with your friends."

Kristen stops laughing and sits up straight. She turns and positions herself so that her left knee is against the back of the seat. She is looking at me. "I want to be with you, Mackenzie. Hanging out with you is the reason I came back here."

All along, I'd hoped that what she is

telling me is the case, but it hadn't been spoken until now. Again, I want to tell her that I want to be more than friends, but the time still doesn't feel right.

But when will it *ever*? I wonder.

Screw it, I decide, and I finally start to get it all off my chest. "I meant what I said earlier…"

Kristen looks at me, confused.

I stumble over my words, but I continue. "About going into the lab to make out…" I realize what I'm saying doesn't really make much sense. "Sorry… I'm… I guess I'm really bad at this," I admit with a chuckle.

She giggles and puts her hand on my shoulder. "I know what you mean."

I finally turn to look at her. "You do?"

She smiles and nods. Our eyes lock, and, after a few seconds, I start to lean toward her. She is mirroring my motions, and I close my eyes. Eventually our lips find each other's, and I don't want to stop.

Then, all of a sudden, something bangs onto the front of the golf cart. The sound scares the crap out of me, and my eyes fly open. Kristen and I both jump back, away from each other. I spin around to see what's happening. It's a person. A girl wearing a hula skirt and a coconut bra.

"Oh my God, I've been looking *everywhere* for you," Tina grabs Kristen's arm and starts to pull her from the seat. "C'mon. I'm about to shotgun my first beer. I don't want you to miss it."

Kristen gives in to the pull of her friend and slides from the seat.

As they are walking away, Tina spins around to look at me. "C'mon, Mackenzie." She motions with her hand for me to join them.

I want to, but I know I can't. Kristen knows too, and when she looks at me, she smiles and shrugs her shoulders.

"I've got to go home," I yell out.

"See you tomorrow," Kristen yells back and lets Tina continue guiding her toward the beach.

When I get home, Dad is waiting on the front porch. I turn into the driveway and notice him look at his watch. I know he's pissed. I park the golf cart underneath the carport and start walking. Normally I'd go in the back door, but I know Dad expects me to meet him at the front. He stands from the chair before I make it to the steps. "I would ask you again where you got the code, but there's only one person on the island other than me that has it, and I've already talked to him."

This is something I hadn't known. I've always thought *nobody* else knew the code to the lab. The only person I can imagine Dad giving it to would be Ryan. I mentally place this new link into the chain of events—if Ryan is the one that Dad entrusted with the code, then, somehow, David got the code from Ryan and eventually passed it off to Brockley.

Dad continues. "He said he didn't give it to you, and I believe him. In fact, he told me somebody went into his house while he was working the other day. When he got home, he noticed a few things had been moved around, but he didn't think anything was missing. So tell me, what are you up to? What were you expecting to find in there?"

"You're wrong." I tell him. "I didn't break into Ryan's house. Besides, what do you have in there that's causing you to be so secretive? What are you hiding?"

"I'm not hiding anything, Mackenzie."

Not hiding anything? That's a joke. "I know about Aunt Sally. I know she's still alive."

Dad stares at me for a moment, takes a deep breath, and returns to his seat. He knows it's time to tell the truth. "A long time ago when I was about your age, my sister made a huge mistake..." He recounts what Loretta already told me—Sally was the mastermind behind a Silas Harrow prank that resulted in the death of a classmate. The plan had been to stage a Silas Harrow sighting, one where he was hanging from the old oak tree in the peach orchard, but the safety harness slipped, and the guy playing Silas succumbed to the rope that was looped around his neck. "Everybody around town blamed Sally for what happened to that kid. As a horrible act of revenge, the kid's father even tried to kill her."

This part is something Loretta *hadn't* mentioned. "Go on," I say.

"He broke into our house one afternoon while she was napping and wrapped an extension cord around her neck. Sally managed to escape, but the man vowed that if he ever saw her again he'd finish what he started that day. As you can imagine, Sally was scared for her life and ran away.

"When you were little," he tells me, "you found a picture of your aunt from when she and I were kids, and you asked me about her—who she was, why you'd never met. Obviously I couldn't even begin to explain the truth of all of that to a five year old, and that's where the lie started. I was going to tell you one day, but the time just never felt right. I'm sorry."

I nod, accepting the apology, and we stay there in silence for a long time.

"So what's going on?" Dad asks. "If you didn't take the code, where did you get it? And you still haven't answered *my* question—Why did you go in there?"

He has been honest with me, so I tell him everything.

CHAPTER FOURTEEN

NOT LONG AFTER daybreak, Dad and I are standing in front of the lab where we're waiting on the officer to arrive. The morning is chilly, and a dense fog lingers close to the ground.

"Storm's coming in," Dad says. "You can feel it in the air."

A group of sea gulls fly over where we're standing, squawking as they pass.

"Even the birds can sense it," he continues. "Things in nature have a way of knowing when to scram."

After our talk the night before, Dad called Officer Wooley first thing this morning. He told her about the break in at Ryan's, the possibility of Brockley being a missing person, and how we know that she and David both had the code to the door.

The wait is excruciating. I'm nervous, and I start to pace back and forth. When I turn the corner of the barn, I spot Ryan in the same garden where Dad got hurt a few days ago. Ryan has a hoe in his hands and is busy clearing weeds from around the Ya-Te-Veo and the other plants of legend. I walk over there.

When Ryan sees me, he stops what he's doing. He stands the hoe upright and props his elbow on the end of the handle. "You're up early," he says.

I don't look at him. Instead, I'm staring at the man-eating tree. The long, thorny fronds remind me of the thing Kristen and I saw in the lab the night before. They make me think of the cell tower and the old illustration of The Vampire Vine that used to give me nightmares.

"Why didn't you tell somebody about your house being broken into?" I ask, quietly, and lean on the fence. "And, no, it wasn't me."

Ryan shrugs his shoulders. "I didn't think anything was missing. I figured it was probably one of the spring breakers looking for beer money, and, believe me, I don't want to get tied up in any of that mess. I've spent enough time around those kinds of crowds to last a life time."

I realize he's right—the partying lifestyle is exactly what he's worked so hard to get away from. His problem was a lot worse than spring break binge drinking, but still. I see his point.

"David had the code," I confess. "And Brockley, too."

The expression on Ryan's face tells me he is surprised about what I'm telling him. He steps toward me and lets the hoe fall to the ground.

"Brockley hasn't been seen or heard from in the past two days," I explain. "This is day three." I look toward the horizon. The sun is higher now, and the fog is lifting. "I already told Dad, and Officer Wooley's on her way to check out the inside of the lab. She'll probably want to talk to you too. About the break in."

Now, Ryan is standing next to me, but on the opposite side of the fence. He leans on the rail, propping himself up with his forearms. We are facing opposite directions. After driving drunk and having a horrible wreck that killed his girlfriend, Ryan escaped his demons and found solace here, and now I'm trying to get away. How can the same place be a respite for one and a thorn for another? "Pretty soon none of this will matter to me," I say. "At the end of this summer, I'm out of here."

I can tell that Ryan is thinking hard about what I'm telling him and about what he's going to say in response. Finally, he nods his head. "It's not going to be any different out there," he confides. "People will be the same. The resort is just a smaller version of the real world. You have to learn to find your place among it all. You have to *make* the life you want."

In the distance, there's the sound of an approaching vehicle. I look up and see a pair of headlights cutting through the still diminishing fog. It is a truck-style utility vehicle that has the word *security* printed on both sides. A row of blue lights stretches across the top of the cab, but they are not flashing. The UTV comes to a stop on the other side of the barn, and Officer Wooley steps out. She has a large travel cup of coffee in her hand. Steam is rising from the cup's lid.

"Well, I might as well go over there and get this over with," I stand up straight and start walking to where Wooley and Dad are already talking.

Officer Wooley is a former deputy from one of the rural counties in South Carolina. She was responsible for nailing a pair of teen murderers a couple of years back. Like our sea captain, Milton, she moved to the resort soon after retiring. I'm sure she's had more than enough of this teen drama crap.

"Mackenzie, what's going on?" Wooley takes a long, slow sip from the cup and then uses her free hand to push back a strand of hair that's come loose from her ponytail. "Your dad says you think Brockley might've gone in there?" She nods toward the door of the lab.

"It makes sense" I say. "She's a botany major, and I'm sure she'd be interested."

"Well, the problem is that we don't have any evidence of foul play. We might find something in there, but so far, nadda." Wooley walks over and places the coffee cup on top of the UTV. Then she turns to look at Dad. "I'm ready when you are, Mr. Walker."

Dad steps forward and unlocks the door. He goes inside and disarms the alarm. The hallway's overhead lights flicker to life, and Officer Wooley steps in first. She leads the way, and Dad and I fall in stride behind her.

Once we get to the solarium, Wooley begins looking everywhere for any sign that Brockley has been there. Dad and I are standing on the opposite side of the space, watching. My eyes scan the room. It all seems so different in the daytime. The sun shining in through the overhead glass takes away almost all of the ominous creep factor that'd been there the night before. I don't see any sign of the monstrous vine, but I do notice something strange—the grated cover of the floor drain is off and lying next to the hole. I start to wonder if the pipe is how the vine found its way in.

As I'm thinking about this, there's the sound of the velvety black curtain being pulled back, and the metallic scrape of the clips along the curtain rod makes my skin crawl. I look up, and Wooley is standing in front of the small room in the corner, observing. When she turns away, I'm able to catch a glimpse of what's on the other side—it's the same chair that'd spooked me and Vinyl four years earlier.

It's funny how some things can seem to haunt you forever. Right now, all of the teasing and bullying that was caused by Vinyl's rumor about Dad feels as fresh as an open wound.

Wooley chuckles, and the sound of her laughter breaks the unwanted memories that are beginning to creep up on me. "What are you doing in here, Mr. Walker? Are you experimenting on plants or *people*?" The statement cuts deep.

Dad stands up straight. "That's from a long time ago," he explains. "I was trying to learn more about plant intelligence. I wanted to link the behavior of plants to the workings of the human brain. Eventually, I just gave up."

After Wooley looks around for a few more minutes, she finally comes over to us. "I don't see anything in here that screams crime scene. I talked to Brockley's roommate, and she told me that Brockley hasn't been getting along with the rest of the girls. She seems to think Brockley has probably been staying with a guy. But if what y'all are telling me is true—that Brockley hooked up with the dead kid—I don't think she's moved on to somebody else that quick. Anyway, with the cell signal being so wonky, trying to call her doesn't help. All I can do is keep looking. For her, or something else."

After we exit the building, Wooley goes over to talk to Ryan. Dad and I are left alone.

I SPEND THE rest of the day working at The Bike Shed.

Mom has made the PR decision for all of us to keep things going as smoothly and normal as possible on the island, as if nothing weird is going on. If word gets out that there is a missing person, people will freak out, and the remainder of the week will be a bust. Not to mention what could happen to the upcoming summer business. The scandal is a risk we can't afford.

Around noon, Kristen comes to hang out and brings me lunch. The day has been slow, and the two of us sit on the end of the dock. Birds circle around and land on the old, lichen-covered posts. Below us, dozens of tiny crabs skitter around on top of the pluff mud. The dark clouds in the sky are increasing, but the rain is holding off.

"Maybe what we saw in the lab wasn't really as bad as we think." I rip into the paper that's wrapped around my sub sandwich. "Maybe the vine wasn't even moving. It could have been a trick of the light. I didn't see anything when we went in there this morning."

Kristen nods her head, going along with what I'm suggesting, but even I realize my words are hollow. I know what I saw.

Just then, I catch movement out of the corner of my eye and see Urchin, Milton's old hound dog, galloping down the dock toward us. He greets both of us with slobbery face kisses and then begins whimpering for us to share our food. We give in and slip him small pieces of lunchmeat.

As we eat, I take Mom's PR suggestion and transform it into my own way of thinking. There are only two more nights of spring break, and I want the time I have left with Kristen to be the best it can be. I want to put everything else aside. "Do you want to hang out tonight?" I ask her.

Kristen has her mouth full and places her sandwich down on its paper. She wipes her hands on a napkin then reaches into her back pocket and pulls out a piece of paper. "That reminds me. Caleb brought these by the campsite." She hands the postcard-sized paper to me.

Grand Finale—The Last Big Party of Spring Break—Hotel Oleander

"Tina wants to go," Kristen says. "I was thinking maybe we could tag along, stay for a little while, and then ditch."

I'm surprised by what she's suggesting. "You want to go to a frat party?"

Kristen shrugs her shoulders. "You know what they say… sooner or later you need to face your fears."

After everything else we've been through, the idea of doing *anything* that's even remotely normal sounds intriguing. Even a frat party. "Yeah, I'd like that."

When we're done eating, Kristen heads back to the beach where she plans on spending a couple of hours laying out in the sun with Tina. Without Kristen's company, the rest of the afternoon drags by. Finally its time to close up shop, and, after everything is squared away, I jump onto my golf cart and drive toward the zip line where I need to finish checking the course for tonight's lighted event.

I decide to swing by the cell tower just to see what the vine situation is like. We haven't had signal all day, so I don't expect it to be clear, but what I see when I get there is completely unexpected.

All of the little pieces that Ryan and I chopped off and threw onto the ground have taken root in the soil. But that's not all—not only have they rooted, they've grown. The cell tower is completely covered. Vines are reaching out in every direction. They're in the trees and running across the ground.

I look at my watch and know I don't have time to start clearing it now. It will be dark in a couple of hours, and I've got time sensitive work to do. I turn the steering wheel on the golf cart, and something on the ground near the edge of the woods catches my eye.

Even from this distance, I can see that it's a blue spiral-bound notebook that's partially covered by vines. I put the cart in park, step out, and slowly walk over the carpet of vegetation. I kneel down and slowly reach my hand into the tangle of vines, careful not to scratch myself on the thorns. Eventually my fingertips brush the book's surface, and I'm able to wrap my hand around the spine. All of a sudden there is a sharp prick on my wrist, and, with the notebook still in my grasp, I jerk my hand back.

When I stand, several pieces of paper fall out and scatter at my feet. I open the notebook and notice Brockley's name has been written in cursive on the inside cover. The notebook is exactly what we've been missing—a piece of evidence in Brockley's disappearance. I bend over and begin picking up the loose pages.

The first paper has a sketched illustration of a girl sitting in an industrial-type chair. Both of the girl's arms are strapped down. There's a metal halo around her head. Several cables run from the halo to the bottom right of the paper where there's a sloppily drawn potted plant. I know for sure that the chair is the same one that's in Dad's lab.

I quickly ruffle through the other papers—there's a map with marked coordinates, a list of seemingly random numbers, HTML code for a computer program, and pages upon pages of scientific jargon that I can't begin to understand. I shove it all back into the notebook and run to the golf cart. I need to get this stuff to Officer Wooley. ASAP.

The golf cart's tires spin as I floor the acceleration pedal. When I emerge from the woods, I hear the unmistakable sound of sirens. Then, a moment later, I see the flashing blue lights. Officer Wooley's UTV is flying down the path on the far side of the land.

I turn my steering wheel sharply to the left and follow her.

CHAPTER FIFTEEN

OFFICER WOOLEY'S UTV is speeding through the wooded land ahead of me. She's swerving left and right, dodging pine trees and deep ruts.

I'm driving as fast as I can to keep up with her, but I'm losing ground. Quickly. It's still a couple of hours till dusk, but this late in the day the woods are already eerie and full of darkness. There's a slight funk in the air, and, under the circumstances, my stomach starts to feel sick.

Wooley comes to a stop in a small clearing. Milton is standing there, and Urchin is sitting on the ground at his side. The dog is looking up and barking at something in the trees.

By the time I get to the scene, Officer Wooley has already stepped out of her UTV and is standing next to the man and his dog. Neither she, Milton, or Urchin acknowledge my arrival. Whatever is above them is far more important. I pull to a stop. The odor is even worse here; it's like something has died. Milton raises his arm and points toward the object of Urchin's unrelenting attention. Wooley follows Milton's lead and tilts her head back to see.

I do too.

The grotesque visage in the trees is awful, sickening, and makes me feel like I might yak. The source of what I'm smelling is now obvious. I turn away, but a moment later I force myself to look again—just to make sure that what I saw is real.

A girl is up there in the branches. Dead. It appears that she is suspended from the tree limbs by a mass of thick vines that are wrapped around her wrists and outstretched arms. The combination of her lifeless body and the flashing blue light from the UTV makes it feel like I'm on a Halloween haunted trail instead of the woods on my family's island resort.

A tangle of green vines are twisted around the girl's neck so tight that her face is blue from strangulation. Her lifeless, glassy eyes are bulging from the sockets. The thorns have cut into her flesh, and blood has dripped down the front of her white button-down shirt where it has dried into a rust colored splotch.

The girl is Brockley.

Officer Wooley pulls the CB radio from her belt clip and turns it on. There is the crackle of the radio coming to life, and I know she's about to call for backup from the mainland.

My heart is hammering in my chest, and I'm starting to feel weak, like I might pass out. I can't believe all of this is happening. This is the second dead body found on the island in the matter of days, and the fact is terrifying.

Out of nowhere, the radio is jerked from Wooley's hand and lands on the ground several feet away. It takes me a second, but I realize what has happened, even though it's hard to believe. One of the vines wrapped itself around the transmitter and yanked it away from her. The vine pulls tighter and crushes the thick plastic in its grip.

All of this makes several things glaringly clear. Now I know Kristen and I weren't imagining things in the lab last night. The vines are real, and they can move. On top of all of that, it appears that the vines are *smart*. They know how to protect themselves.

From my left, Urchin barrels past, barking his head off. The abrupt sound causes me to jump, and I realize that the dog has pulled the leash out of his master's hand. As the leash zips past where I'm standing, I reach for the handle, but it slips through my fingers.

Urchin is several yards in front of us now, barking and growling at the moving vine. Finally the tendril comes loose from the CB. A second later Urchin cries out, and I know that one of the thorns has gotten him on the nose.

Urchin turns from us and hightails it into the woods. Milton runs after his beloved pet, yelling for him to come back.

I'm watching the pair disappear into the trees when Officer Wooley speaks up. "It got me on the hand," she says from right beside me. I look, and her hand is smeared with blood. I realize that when the vine yanked the radio, it must have sliced into her.

"How bad is it?" I ask.

She holds her hand up. The laceration is pretty deep across her palm, but it doesn't look like she'll need stitches. I take off my shirt and wrap it around her hand, pulling the fabric tight. The pressure should stop the blood flow.

"I've got to get in touch with the deputies," she says and uses her left hand to reach into the front pocket of her pants for her phone. "We're going to need help." When she has the phone out, she starts to dial. "Shit. No signal."

I'm not surprised, but my heart drops, and I look toward the danger that is unfurling in front of us. The vines are slowly creeping toward us from all directions. I remember the image of the cell tower from earlier, and I realize that the vines have intentionally cut off all communication from the island.

"We've got to get out of here," I say.

We start to hurry back, and I'm stopped dead in my tracks when I notice the front wheels on my golf cart are slowly turning toward the right. The suspension and axles squeal and pop. It only takes a second to see what's going on. One of the vines has wrapped itself around the steering wheel. Other vines are on the vehicle body, and all of them begin to pull. The golf cart tilts sideways and starts to slide away from where we're standing.

"This one's clear," Wooley yells from behind me, referring to her own UTV. I hear the engine start, and she drives around so that she is in between me and the other cart. "Get in," she says.

I can't. Not yet. Brockley's notebook was left on the seat of my ride. At first I'd thought it was just a piece of evidence in Brockley's whereabouts, but now I'm positive the notebook and the papers inside hold the key to what's going on with the vines. We'll need the information if we're ever going to escape this nightmare.

I run around Wooley's UTV. The other golf cart is completely on its side now and is inching across the ground, cutting deep into the dirt. The underside is facing me, and I run up to it. With my hands on the edge, I look over the side, but I don't see the notebook. When the golf car flipped over, the notebook must've fallen out. That means it's probably wedged beneath the weight of the fiberglass and metal.

"Get in, Mackenzie!" Officer Wooley yells out again from behind me.

"Wait," I say, "there's something here that we need."

I've spotted the notebook now, and I drop to my knees. It's underneath the bulky equipment, and I use my hands to simultaneously tug on the notebook and claw at the dirt beneath it. I almost have the notebook free when the golf cart stops moving, and I look up.

The width of the body is only like four feet, but I know if it topples over on me I would easily be hurt, maybe even crushed. There's a creaking sound, and the whole thing starts to wobble. I yank the notebook as hard as I can, and it comes free, but the force of my tugging sends me flat on my ass. The golf cart starts falling toward me, and I scramble backward and manage to get out of the way just before the nine hundred pounds crash onto the ground inches from my feet.

I take a moment to let the reality of my

safety settle. The vines tried to kill me, I realize, and I take a deep breath.

"Okay, you're coming with me," Officer Wooley demands. "Now." My mind had been so focused on the task of rescuing the notebook that I'd forgotten that somebody else was in the woods with me. The sound of her voice is a relief, and it makes me happy.

I get to my feet and take a seat next to Wooley in the UTV. She immediately starts to drive away from the clearing. She's already turned off the blue lights, but the UTV's headlights cut through the darkness of the woods and send spooky shadows into the landscape.

"What were those things?" Officer Wooley asks and glances in the small rearview mirror at what we're leaving behind. "And what is *that*?" She turns her focus toward the notebook in my lap.

I tell her the notebook belonged to Brockley, and that I found it in the woods earlier that evening when I'd gone to check the zip line.

Crap. The zip line. "We've got to turn around," I say. "There's supposed to be a lighted event tonight. People can't go in the woods, not with the vines. They'll be in danger. We have to find Tyler. He's the one that supposed to be in charge of driving them out there."

Without any further discussion, Wooley loops the UTV around and picks up the sandy road that leads toward the side of the island where Tyler's small apartment is located. It is a several minute drive to get there, and Wooley returns to her topic of conversation. "So, the notebook," she says, demanding an explanation.

"I'm not sure what all of it means, but we're about to find out. As soon as we're done with Tyler, take me home."

My thoughts travel back to the old, clothbound copy of *The Island of Doctor Moreau* that I'd found in Dad's childhood home. I've read the book before, for school, and I know that one of the themes of the short sci-fi novel is the dangers that come with playing God. In the book, Moreau's creations of animal and human hybrid begin to fight back against him and the rest of the island.

In my mind, I link the knowledge of the book's events with that of Dad experimenting with plants. Dad said he'd been searching for the link between plant intelligence and the human brain. Had he found it? And, if so, what had he done with the data? Had he spliced the two things together? Are the vines somehow a result of his meddling in nature?

The whole concept of what I'm thinking gives me chills, but, in some kind of weird and outlandish way, it makes sense. I have a feeling that if it's all looked at under the right viewpoint, everything inside Brockley's notebook will tie all of this together. Dad, Aunt Sally, Loretta, David, Brockley, and whatever's going on with the vines are all interwoven. I'm sure of it, and it's time to demand answers.

CHAPTER SIXTEEN

"DAD, WHAT IS this?" I drop the notebook onto the patio table in front of him. It's already pitch black outside. The porch light is off on account of nesting sea turtles, but I know the dim amber glow that's coming from the window behind him is enough to see by.

After Officer Wooley and I located Tyler and told him that the twilight zip line is cancelled—we blamed it on the approaching storms, *not* the death of another spring breaker—the two of us arrived at the house a few minutes later. Mom was sitting on the living room sofa, putting the final touches on her painting. It was rare to see her so relaxed and taking a break, but other than the zip line event, the night was done. She jumped up when she saw Wooley's bandaged, bloody hand and my dirt-smeared, bare torso.

"Oh my God. Mackenzie, what happened?" Mom's mouth dropped open, and her eyes shot back and forth from Officer Wooley to me.

"We're okay," I assured her. "Where's Dad?" I went to the backdoor to grab a jacket from the coat rack on the wall and spotted him sitting on the porch with a glass of whiskey in his hand. I pulled on the jacket—not because I was cold, just that I needed something to cover my top half—and went out there to join him.

"Open it," I say and nod my head toward Brockley's notebook. I pull the front zipper up on the jacket. The jacket is one of my favorites—dark blue with a single red stripe down each sleeve. Wearing it now is a strange piece of comfort in an otherwise dreadful situation.

After Dad takes a sip from his drink, he puts the glass back on the table, spins the notebook around so that it is facing him the correct way, and opens the front cover.

"It belonged to the missing girl," I start to explain.

"The *dead* girl." It's Officer Wooley that points out the important, sinister detail of what's happened. She and Mom are standing behind me. I hadn't even known that they'd followed me outside, and the sound of the officer's voice takes me by surprise.

Officer Wooley tells Dad how Milton was walking Urchin through the woods earlier in the evening and came across Brockley's lifeless body stuck up there in the trees.

Dad turns his attention away from the three of us and back to the notebook, flipping through the pages. I watch his face, waiting for any tell-tell signs that he knows all the answers to what's happening. The expression on his face is one of alarm.

"I think maybe you were right. David Fiske didn't die from playing the choking game," I say. "Something else is going on. And this other girl, Brockley, was somehow involved. But I don't understand... why would you have thought that Silas Harrow had anything to do with it?"

I can see how Brockley and David's deaths could possibly be connected to one another, but the idea that the legend of Silas has anything to do with what happened to the two teenagers on the island still throws me for a loop.

"When David was found dead the other day, I was sure that the kid's father finally snapped after all these years and came to the island. I thought that by killing someone here in the same way that his son died, by choking, was a way that he thought he would be able to get me to confess Sally's location. I went back to Trenton looking for answers, but now, this... " he motions to the open notebook with his hand, "I know that I was wrong. This has nothing to do with Silas Harrow or Sally's prank from twenty years ago. Something else is going on.

Something far *worse*." He pauses.

Officer Wooley steps forward. "What is it, Mr. Walker?" She asks, urging him on.

"It's going to take me a few minutes to figure out the exact logistics, but I think I've got the gist of it from this one page," he says.

I glance down and see the page that he is referring to. It is the one that has the map with all of the marked coordinates.

Dad's phone is sitting on the table next to the half-empty glass of whiskey. He picks up the phone and turns it on. There's no wi-fi, but he doesn't need it for what he is showing me. "This is a PDF map of the island's current layout." He flips the phone around so that the three of us can see. Mom and Officer Wooley step closer. The varying landscape patterns are marked on the map—triangles are there for the woods, x's for areas of lawn, dots for sand, and wavy lines for water. All of the buildings are sketched at their appropriate location in conjunction with everything else that is around them.

Dad places the phone face-up on the table and pulls the paper map from the inside pages of Brockley's notebook. "Look at what's marked," he says and points to the small pinpoints of red ink that are on the graph paper. "The coordinates match up with each of the hotels on the resort."

He flips to another page in the notebook. It is the page with the all of the scientific wording. "Somebody has used my years of extensive research and is now controlling the vines... "

"What do you mean, *the vines*?" Officer Wooley asks.

Dad takes a deep sigh and then tells us. "Years ago, after certain articles were published about my close attempts at linking the human brain to plant intelligence, I was contacted and commissioned by the government. With their backing and lots of trial and error, I was able to create a new variety of plant that could be controlled by human thoughts. The ultimate goal was to make it so the vines could be used to work farmland. From a central location, one person would be able to do the work of an entire crew, sowing and harvesting without the added expense of additional labor. Imagine up to thirty acres of peaches being picked by the outreaching vines from one single plant."

I'd seen the way the vine wrapped itself around Officer Wooley's CB radio in the woods and can easily picture several of the vines stretched down the length of each row in a field, doing something similar with the fruits and vegetables.

"This island was the test location for the project," Dad says and then pauses. He runs his hand through his thinning hair. "In the end, we lost the grant, and the whole thing fell apart."

But the vines stayed, I realize.

From this point in his story, Dad stands up and starts pacing the patio. The sky flashes with lightning, and there's the distant rumble of thunder. So far today we've dodged each of the storms, but I have a feeling we won't miss this one. Dad walks to the edge of the patio, pauses for a few seconds, and then turns around so that he is facing us again. "Somebody is controlling every move the vines make. They're planning to use the vines to attack the hotels."

I remember the flyer Kristen showed me when we'd been having lunch together on the marina's dock earlier in the day. "There's a huge party at Oleander tonight," I say. "There's going to be a *ton* of people there." Thankfully, Kristen was going to wait on me before she headed over, and I don't have to worry about her being among the crowd.

The day before, Kristen and I had seen broken ground outside the same hotel. It was the vines that were already beginning to push through the dirt. Once it starts in earnest, the whole building could be destroyed in a matter of minutes. And if the building is full of drunk college students and teenagers, the result could be catastrophic.

"Is it possible to know where the attack it is being orchestrated *from*?" Officer Wooley asks.

"Originally, the control center was in the lab, but that's not the case now." Dad walks back to the table and leans over the map. "But lucky for us, whoever is behind the whole thing has marked the place of origin." His index finger lands on one of the red dots on the map. "It's in the woods," he says. "The electrical shed behind the cell tower. If I hurry, maybe I can get there in time." He closes the notebook, throws back the rest of his whiskey, and starts to descend the patio steps.

"I'm going, too." Officer Wooley moves forward.

"No," Dad tells her. "You're hurt," pointing out the obvious.

At the edge of the patio, Officer Wooley stops walking and stands still. I can tell that she knows he's right. She should stay behind, but she wants to help. She's been protecting people for so long it is like second nature to her.

"If I'm not going with you, I'll go to Hotel Oleander," she says. "I'll get everybody out. I'll make sure they get to safety."

I glance at my watch. The party's already started, and I know it's going to be an enormous task trying to clear the place. "You go with Officer Wooley, Mom. She's going to need help."

Mom shakes her head. "I'm not leaving you here by yourself, Mackenzie."

"You won't be," I tell her. "I'm going with Dad. The woods are covered in vines. The zip line will be the easiest way to get where we need to be, and I'm the best at it."

CHAPTER SEVENTEEN

THE LITTLE CINDERBLOCK building behind the cell tower is always kept locked, and I know Ryan has a key. I realize now that whoever broke into Ryan's cottage a few days ago was after more than the code to the lab.

I remember seeing Ryan coming out of the shed. I'd been out there clearing the cell tower of kudzu, and he appeared from inside the building, taking me by surprise. Obviously, there was nothing inside the building then that's related to what's happening now, but the timeline matches up. Whoever is responsible—presumably a spring breaker—arrived on the island, broke into Ryan's house, and took what they needed, the code and the key. This person then went into Dad's lab, stole *his* information, and then set the whole thing in motion.

Dad is behind the wheel of his golf cart, and I'm sitting next to him in the passenger seat. He's driving as fast as he can, and we jostle over the rough terrain. The room lights of Hotel Oleander are visible through the trees, and, intermingled with thumping country music, there is the occasional eruption of loud, jubilant laughter that travels all the way from the hotel to where we are.

The far-off sights and sounds are a reminder of everything that's at stake. According to what we found in Brockley's notebook, somebody is intentionally targeting the hotel. Somebody that seems to have a grudge against the sorority and fraternity. This person knows about the big bash that's happening there tonight and sees it as the perfect opportunity to strike.

If the situation was even slightly different I would be positive that Brockley was the one behind the evil act. She had motivation to kill David, and we know that she was viewed as an outcast by the rest of the sorority sisters. Maybe Brockley had reached a point where she'd finally had enough and decided it was time for payback. The vines would be a way to settle the score with most of SCU's Greek system all at once. It makes sense, but the idea is fruitless. After all, it can't be Brockley—she's dead.

Dad hits a deep hole in the land, and I bounce high enough from my seat that I bump my head on the top of the golf cart. In an attempt to steady myself, I grab onto the handrail next to me.

Who else on the island, aside from Brockley, would have a strong enough agenda to kill these people? I think about David and

Brockley and try to connect others to the two of them, but still I come up empty handed. There has to be somebody else that's angry at the organizations. From what I've seen, sorority life can be like an exclusive club that, once you get in, forces you to conform to what they want... or else. Look at what happened to Kristen's sister—she was kicked out.

Then it hits me. It's a realization that I don't want to be having, but why hadn't I thought about it earlier? Kristen told me one time that Allison was pissed after she was expelled from the sorority. My stomach flips at what I'm starting to think is a very real possibility. Is it possible that Allison could have been angry enough about what happened to her that she would kill people?

After Allison was voted out of the sorority, she didn't come back to the resort again. Therefore she can't be the one behind what's going on... unless she sent somebody else to do the dirty work for her.

The golf cart skids to a stop within a small clearing in the woods. Overhead, several strands of string lights run the length of the zip line. The lights are turned on, and the multitude of them gives a golden glow to our surroundings. It's clear that there's not any vines in the immediate vicinity of where we are, but there *is* creeping movement deeper within the darkness of the trees, and I know that they're out there. Not only can I catch glimpses of the vines twisting and unfurling through the tree branches, I can hear them brushing past leaves and against rough tree bark.

Out here, the horrid stench is stronger than it was before. I'm reminded of the gruesome scene of Brockley's dead body and remember where the odor is coming from. Thinking about all of this makes me have to hold my breath for a moment. I cover my mouth and nose with the front of my jacket.

"It's the corpse flower," Dad says.

I turn to look at him and speak from behind the fabric. "It's blooming *now*?" There is only one of the carrion flowers on the island, the one in Dad's garden, and it has only bloomed once in my lifetime. When a corpse flower opens, the smell that it emits is close to the stench of decaying flesh. The odor is a way for the plant to attract flies and other insects that will serve as pollinators.

"The strain of vine that we're dealing with has been spliced with the corpse flower," Dad tells me. "There's actually several dozen of the flowers that could push through the ground any minute now."

I take a moment to let what he's telling me sink in. The vines are only a small part of a much larger specimen—a plant that once it pollinates is going to spread.

I get out of the golf cart first, and Dad follows close behind. We get our harnesses from below the seat, put them on, and together we walk toward the tall oak tree that this particular platform has been build around.

The platform's surface is at least twenty feet off the ground. This isn't one of the main checkpoints of the zip line, so we've never taken the time to build steps leading up to it. The small platform is accessible only by a vertical wooden ladder.

Climbing ladders this tall can be scary if you're not used to it, but I've done it so many times that I think nothing of it. One hand over the other, step up, repeat, and don't look down.

Once we get to the top of the ladder and both of us are standing on the floor, I secure each of our harnesses to the line. Out of the corner of my eye, I see Hotel Oleander go dark. Then it's the string lights, leaving us without light. The power has gone out all over the resort. The outage is followed by an exclamation from the crowd of partiers. It's like the sound you hear in a crowded shopping mall after there's been a loud clap of thunder.

"We've got to hurry," I tell Dad. "Wait until I'm on the next platform before you go."

I turn around and step off. The feeling I get from flying through the air isn't the same as it normally is. Gone are the usual sensations of freedom and exhilaration; they've been replaced by nerve-racking dread and urgency. I try not to, but I look down and see thick patches of coiling vine below me.

My feet land on the next platform. This one is the closest to the cell tower and the outbuilding. Dad lands on the floor not long after me, and I unfasten both of our vests. We're a good twenty yards away from where we have to go, but there's a clear path. The cell tower is completely covered, but most of the vines are not reaching toward the small building that's behind it. Like a common houseplant's natural instinct of growing toward sunlight for the nourishment that it needs to survive, the vines are reaching for what they are being guided to do... kill spring breakers.

"If we hurry, we should be able to get down there with plenty of time," I say. "The trick is going to be getting back up here before the vines have completely blocked our path."

We've seen it happen already. Once the vines realize what we've come to do, they will react accordingly.

We rush down the steps and run across the open space. When we're there, Dad pulls a flashlight from the waistband of his jeans and turns it on. He shines the light toward the structure, and it lands on the open door. As we move forward, I'm able to catch glimpses of what's inside. Bundled and zip-tied cables and wires are running across the concrete floor. A metal folding chair sits in the middle of the room, but it's empty. Well, not entirely. There is an open laptop computer on the seat. From the USB port, there is a thick bundle of red and black wires that trails off into the dark corner at the back of the room, and then the whole thing runs through a hole that's been drilled into the concrete.

The computer's power cord is plugged into the wall socket, but now that the power is out on the island, the device is running on battery.

Dad steps inside the building, leaving me outside the door. He kneels down in front of the computer and touches the mouse pad. The monitor comes alive.

The screen is white and has a seemingly

endless series of letters and numbers scrolling up from the bottom. I don't know a lot about computers, but I know that what I'm seeing is some type of code.

Dad promptly lifts the computer from the seat of the chair and jerks the USB cable from its side. Then he pulls his arm back and throws the laptop hard against the cinderblock wall where it crashes and then clatters to the floor. The computer lands so that the cover is facing me. There's a sticker on the flat surface that catches my eye. It is something I've seen before. A wagon wheel. Not only that, there are initials— D.F. The person responsible has been right under our nose all along. David Fiske.

When I'd looked at David's social media several days ago I'd thought it was odd that he went from being a geeky sci-fi fan to a frat boy in the matter of months, but I decided that maybe he'd simply changed. People do.

Now I can see the glaring truth. David joined the fraternity for a singular, hateful purpose—to kill them. David, the smart computer nerd, wrote a very specific HTML code that could program the plant to do his bidding. Dad's government-backed plan of creating a plant that can be controlled by human thoughts has evolved into something else entirely. Even if David is the one responsible for the techno-botanical hybrid, it still doesn't explain his *own* death.

From the other side of the wall I hear movement. It sounds like tree branches scratching against the cinderblock surface. I peek around the corner. Vines are starting to move around the narrow building from both sides. Visually, it's almost like long fingers are wrapping themselves around the structure.

"Dad, you've got to get out of there," I warn him.

He steps through the door just in time. From behind him comes a cracking sound, and I know what's about to happen. Under the pressure of the twisting and tightening vines, the little building falls in on itself. Dust flies up, and the pieces of cinderblock and metal are pulled into the depth of the forest.

Dad and I run to the same platform that we'd climbed down from and ascend the steps. The vines are creeping up behind us. Once we get to the top, I throw Dad's harness over his shoulders and then put on mine. After I have Dad clipped to the line, I gently push him forward "Go," I say. He looks at me, and our eyes lock. "Please, Dad. You go first."

He turns away from me and steps off. I

watch him sail across the space, and then I hear the thump of his boots on the next landing spot. He turns around to look at me and motions with his hand for me to come. I step forward and test my harness to make sure it's secure. I'm about to step off the boards when the zip line cable that's directly ahead of me is ripped down from the trees. There's a forceful tug on my vest that almost causes me to lose my balance, but I manage to unclip the carabiner from the cable and steady myself just in time.

"Dad, go!" I yell across the width. The line that *could* connect us is gone. "Hurry! I'm going to go the other way!" I use my thumb to point over my shoulder toward the opposite zip line. "Get the golf cart and meet me at the beach campsite!"

Eventually Dad follows my instructions. From the distance, I can see him step off the platform. He glides along the line, getting further away every second and finally disappears into the darkness of the trees.

I move to the other end of the floor, and I'm about to clip myself onto the west-facing cable when I hear something snap. Like the one on the other side, this cable has been pulled loose, and it whips past my up-stretched hands. I duck my head down to dodge the line as it comes down.

After I stand up straight, I spin around, looking at the resort below me. The power is out everywhere, but there is the flicker and hum of generators coming from all directions. Rising above the hum is the occasional human scream. I see a steady flashing blue light near Hotel Oleander and know that it is Officer Wooley's UTV; she and Mom made it there safely. Milton's boat is not tied down at the marina, and my eyes scan the horizon, searching for the vessel. When I finally spot it, I immediately know that it is useless. The boat has been demolished to a pile of debris that is drifting out to sea.

Now the vines are reaching above some of the tallest palm and pine trees, twisting toward the nearly full moon. I hear the pop of branches and the gunshot-like snap of whole trees being broken in half. Somewhere in the distance is a deep, steady rumble, and I'm not sure if it's the sound of thunder or an echo of things falling that I'm hearing. It is evident to me now that all of this is far worse than we imagined. The threat is no longer contained to the hotels.

The entire resort is in danger. All of it has become a swirling chaos of plant and terror.

CHAPTER EIGHTEEN

WHEN I WAS younger, I found a sketched picture of Nicaragua's infamous Vampire Vine tacked to the wall in Dad's lab. The image was that of a terrified young woman being restrained by thorny tendrils.

The picture gave me nightmares. Many nights I would have dreams where a thick vine was wrapping itself tight around my neck, and I'd wake up gasping for air and scratching at my throat.

After my friend, Vinyl, started the rumor that Dad was making monsters on the island, my classmates started picking on me and the nightmares intensified. Both scenarios—the waking world and the land of dreams—got so bad that I started to anticipate each of them with an equal amount of dread. Back then, I would have done anything to never have to face those school bullies *or* the nightmarish vines ever again.

Now, it is all closing in on me. From where I'm standing on the zip line's platform, I survey the ground that's in my immediate vicinity, looking for the best route to get myself out of the woods.

A small concrete pad has been left behind

on the ground where the cinderblock building stood. I spot something lying cattycorner next to the foundation—it's the ax that Ryan was using to chop the vines from the cell tower a few days earlier. The ax is the closest thing to a weapon that I see, and my mind starts to work in rapid fire for a way to use it as a means of escape.

There's a several-foot-wide path that the dragging of the cinderblock cut through the bramble. All of the other directions are thick with vine cover. The newly cleared path will be my best bet. Plus, the path leads eastward, toward the beach. If I'm able to get to the campsite in time, hopefully I'll be able to find Kristen and Dad and make sure we all get out of this alive.

I know the layout of the land like it's the back of my hand. There's no visible sign of the building from where I'm standing, so depending on how far the vines have dragged it, I should have a decent length of cleared land to travel. Regardless of how deep into the woods the path actually goes, it will undoubtedly make for the shortest distance to get out of here.

One of the vines reaches over the edge of the platform and starts to inch toward where I'm standing. It doesn't take me but a second to realize that more of them are behind that one, and several of the tendrils are already beginning to wrap around the railing. The section of rail that they're clinging to is the one I found loose a few days earlier and never made it back to secure. The rail topples over from the pull of the vines. I've seen the damage the vines can do and know I have to get down from here. Right now.

After moving to the edge of the platform, I spin around, squat down low, and grab onto the end of the floor boards. I let myself step off backward, and then hold myself suspended in the air. My biceps strain, and the muscles in my back are pulled taught and start to burn. I know I can't hold myself up much longer.

There's a support cable that runs at a perpendicular angle from the corner of the platform all the way to an anchor that's been twisted deep into the ground. I still have my safety harness on, and I think I'll be able to clip the carabiner onto the cable. I reach as far as I can with my right hand, grab onto the edge of the floor boards, and then do the same with my left, moving toward the corner of the platform several inches at a time. Once I'm there, it's a tight reach to get the clip onto the support cable, but I manage to twist my body around just so.

When I let go of the floor boards, my body spins around, and I nearly bang my head against the sharp corner, but my weight causes me to drop just in time to miss. I slide down the cable at a freefall speed, but the angle actually turns out to be perfect and I land on my feet then take a soft fall to my knees.

After I get the clip undone, I run to where the building stood and pick up the ax. Standing on the concrete pad, I take a second to stare off into the woods. The path is still clear, and I can see the rubble of cinderblock up ahead. I was right—the debris is so far away from where I'm standing that I know there won't be too much ground to cover on the other side between it and the beach. From here on, getting out of the woods should be no problem, and I start running.

I don't get far before I hear something moving through the woods on my right. It sounds like a large animal charging through the trees, and it's headed in my direction. In addition to the sound of the fast-paced movement it's making, there's an audible growl, almost human-like. Just when I think the creature—whatever it is—is about to be on top of me, I hear a panicked male voice, "Help me! Somebody, please!"

Before I have time to register what's going on, a body is jerked from the trees. The guy is on his back and being dragged across the ground. Finally, I notice the vine that's wrapped around his arm, pulling him. I lock eyes with the victim—it's Caleb. This is the first time I've seen him not wearing the beer-case cowboy hat, and I logically assume that he's lost it somewhere along the way. Caleb's body is scratched and bloody from where he's been pulled through briars and bramble. He reaches his spare hand toward me, and I run as fast as I can to get to him.

When I get there, I wrap my hand around his. I pull with all of my might, but the opposing strength of the vine is stronger than I am. We are stuck in a deadly tug of war, and, despite my best efforts, I'm losing.

Then, something wraps itself around my calf. I look down and see one of the vines has me in its grasp. For the first time, I feel the true strength of the plant as it begins to pull me away from Caleb.

I try to remain upright as long as I can, but eventually I fall flat on my face into the dirt. Caleb's hand begins slipping out of mine. I try to keep my grip on him as long as I can, but it is only a matter of seconds before our contact breaks.

Without the hold of Caleb, I'm moving

backward across the ground at a much faster speed. My left hand is gripped tight around the handle of the ax. It hasn't rained on the island in a while, and the drag of my body is kicking up a lot of sandy dust. I close my eyes against the assault. The grit is so bad that I can feel it in my mouth. Soon, the smoothness of the path gives way to the rougher, unharmed ground of the forest.

Caleb has completely disappeared into the opposite line of trees. His screams become lower the further away we get from one another until, eventually, I can't hear them at all.

I know I have to act quickly, and I use my free hand to grab onto the nearest tree that I'm being pulled past. It's an oak sapling that's small enough I'm able to wrap my hand all the way around its trunk. The pull of the vine doesn't relent, and soon my grip on the tree is broken. Now, I'm reaching and grabbing at the ground, at anything that could buy me some time. But I'm not able to find a lifeline soon enough, and, a second later, I feel myself being lifted into the air by my leg.

It doesn't take long for my body to leave the ground completely, and I'm hanging upside down. I'm still holding onto the ax for dear life. Blood rushes to my head. It's a sensation I've always hated. It makes me feel woozy. The vine moves me through the air and finally stops so that I'm dangling above something I know can be the end of me.

Directly below my feet is a thick, churning mass of the thorn covered vines. Inside the spiraling chaos is a blue fraternity t-shirt that's ripped and covered in blood. And I see Caleb's bent and torn cowboy hat. There's a hand that breaks the surface, and, as the vines churn, I realize the arm isn't connected to a body.

The vine around my ankle unfurls, and I fall, landing on my back. The heavy cover of vegetation cushions the landing, but the sharp thorns jab into me. Instinctively, I scream out in pain, but I can't allow myself to wallow in the misery. If I just lie here, I'll be consumed. I have to get up.

I start to get to my feet and use my right hand to search for a place among the vines where there are no thorns, a spot that I can grab onto for balance. My hand lands on something soft, and I jerk back, catching a glimpse of what I've touched. There's blood matted fur within the vines, and it's not just a wild animal that's been trapped. I see a collar with a name printed on it—Urchin.

There's no time to dwell on the horrific images that I'm seeing all around me. Other vines are starting to wrap themselves around my legs. I have to fight. I raise the ax and bring it down on top of the first vine—once, twice, three times—eventually chopping it in two.

My attack is relentless, and I start to move forward. The vines are tangled around my feet, but I kick and swing the ax until I tumble free from the deadly bramble, landing on my hands and knees. While I'm on the ground, I spin around so that I'm on my ass, and I crawl away backward from the living nightmare that I somehow managed to escape.

The spot on the ground is a clear sandy patch that's next to a palm tree. It's a place I'm able to pause and collect myself. I drop the ax into the sand and take a moment to catch my breath. Both the harness and my jacket are ripped from where I landed on the thorns. Underneath the layers, my flesh is lacerated and bleeding. I'm in a lot of pain, but I know staying here will do no good for me *or* anybody else.

The beach is not far away. I know I'll feel safer once I make it to where there are other people. I've never really thought that much about the old saying of *safety in numbers*, but, now, I see the point. We're all in this together.

I need to get to the campsite and find Kristen. I need to know that she's okay. Plus, Dad is supposed to be meeting me there with the golf cart. Since Dad and I have a good idea of what's going on, we have a hand up on the situation. The rest of the island needs us. On trembling legs, I get to my feet and pick up the ax again.

CHAPTER NINETEEN

WHEN I EMERGE from the woods, the campsite is stretched out in front of me. It's obviously been abandoned, but a staggered row of tiki torches are still burning. The flicker of orange flame gives enough light for me to see the ground that I'm walking on. The tide is coming in, and the white capped waves are washing all the way up the shore to where a bright red cooler has been left behind.

The toe of my boot hits something and sends it clattering across the wet sand. I look down and see countless plastic cups are scattered around me. Obviously there's been some major pre-gaming going on before tonight's big party, The Grand Finale, but where did everybody go? More specifically, where is Kristen? And what about Mom and Dad?

The wind picks up, and the small flames on top of the torches bend sideways. The plastic cups tumble and roll across the ground. I feel drops of water hitting my face and realize that it's starting to rain. Sharp bolts of lightning are coming down over the ocean. The storm is getting close.

From here, the quickest way to get to the house is to follow the beach to where it loops around by the marina. I start walking in that direction and stop when I'm near the campsite's tents and yurts. There's movement in the shadowy darkness. At first it startles me, but then I realize that what I'm seeing is only a string of dark lights that is swaying back and forth. Some of the vinyl window flaps on the tents have been left undone, and they're whipping in the wind.

The entire campsite has been taken over with vines.

Something brushes against my leg, and it scares the crap out of me. I kick at it, but it's only a piece of dried seaweed that has washed ashore. The wind gets in it and carries it further down the beach.

I turn around and continue the trek toward the marina. I'm the only one out here, and the nighttime walk along the beach is eerie with the brewing storm on the horizon and the distant sound of people screaming. I thought that a throng of people who were looking for a way off the island would have headed toward the marina, but I was wrong.

The beach takes a sharp curve to the left and eventually leads to the inlet where Milton's boat is usually moored. My feet fall into the softer, dry sand, and I make my way to the narrow boardwalk that will take me to the gravel road.

I crest the highest point of the boardwalk, and, when I start to walk downhill, I spot somebody standing up ahead of me. My heart skips, and I stop walking. I grip the ax tighter, just in case.

From here, the figure is only a dark silhouette. "Mackenzie?" He calls my name. I recognize the voice. It is Ryan. I feel a deep sense of relief that he's out here with me, and I relax the arm that's got the ax so that it's straight down my side. I practically run to reach the end of the boardwalk where he's standing. "Ryan, what are you doing out here? It's not safe…"

Ryan grabs me by the forearm. "I know," he says. "I was on my way out when I spotted you. C'mon." He starts to lead me away.

I don't have time to think about or contemplate where we're going. Ryan guides me across the gravel lot, closer to the dock.

"I need to make sure Kristen, Dad, and Mom are okay," I tell him.

"Going with me will be safer than trying to go back. I'm taking the boat to the mainland."

I've already seen Milton's boat demolished and drifting out to sea, and I'm about to tell Ryan that fact when I see what he has in mind. Dad's own boat is bobbing out in the water. The motorboat is small, but it's big enough to hold ten or so passengers.

It's almost done, I think. Just thirty more minutes, and Ryan and I will arrive on the mainland. From there, we'll be able get help.

We're at the end of the dock, and Ryan steps over the side of the boat. I follow behind him, and he is already untying the rope. He doesn't take time to secure it. Instead, he just drops the rope haphazardly at his feet.

I sit down and place the ax on the floor, blade-side down, when I hear people screaming somewhere behind me. The screams are a lot closer than the others I'd been hearing, and I jerk my head around to see. A group of frat guys explode from the woods. I stand. "Over here!" I yell and start motioning for them to come.

They have spotted us. The entire crowd is running toward the marina.

Ryan kicks the boat off the edge of the dock.

I spin around to look at him. "What are you doing? We need to get as many people on here as possible."

Either Ryan doesn't hear what I'm saying or he's ignoring me. He starts the motor.

"Ryan, stop. There are people out there.

We have room." I'm pointing at the empty seats across from me.

In the disappearing landscape, the frat guys are standing on the edge of the boat dock, yelling for us to turn around.

"I don't care about them," Ryan says. "Those kinds of guys are precisely what's wrong with society."

I start to say something, but my mouth just hangs open. I'm speechless and confused about what he's saying. This is not the same Ryan that I've come to know. My heart is hammering behind my ribcage. "What... What are you talking about?"

He steps closer to me, picks up the ax, and tosses it over the edge of the boat where it splashes into the water. "Last year, when I had the wreck, it was a frat boy that was driving the other car that killed my girlfriend."

But Ryan was the one that was drunk. The wreck was *his* fault. In Ryan's warped mind, he's placing the blame on somebody else for his own mistakes.

The wind gets in Ryan's shirt, and I'm able to catch a glimpse of something I'd never seen before. Right below his collar bone is a tattoo like David's—a wagon wheel. It's dark out here on the water, but there's a glimmer of moonlight that reflects off the cross around his neck. The shimmer gets my attention, and I notice that in addition to the gold, he's wearing a second chain. This one has a USB drive dangling from the end. The drive is in a waterproof sleeve.

"Because of people like them, the whole world has gone to shit." Ryan's eyes lock with mine. "But I have the answer right here." He wraps his hand around the USB.

As he's talking, I'm piecing all of this together in my mind. Ryan and David were part of some kind of secret society—a dangerous and deadly one. The jump drive holds the computer program that David wrote for the plants. We'd thought that David's goal was to execute an attack on the party, but Ryan's intentions are on a much grander scale. He plans on taking the USB to the mainland and using the computer program to orchestrate a horrifying agenda based solely on ridiculous stereotypes and generalizations. But I still don't *completely* understand...

"Did you kill David?" I ask.

Ryan nods. "David was one of the best computer programmers out there. I lucked up when I found him. But I figured he'd eventually slip."

Trying to figure out who could have gotten into the fraternity party on the night of David's death has been a tricky question all along. I knew that an adult would have stuck out like a sore thumb, but Ryan isn't much older than us. He could have gone in without anybody thinking anything about it.

"And Brockley?"

Ryan smiles at the mention of her name. The jovial response is unexpected and sinister. "Brockley was an intelligent girl. *Too* smart, really. When she found out what I was doing, she almost brought the whole thing crashing down."

I'd assumed that whoever broke into Ryan's house took the code to the lab, but I realize now that wasn't the case. Ryan gave the code to David so he could steal Dad's research. Brockley was suspicious of what was going on, and she's the one that broke into Ryan's, looking for proof.

"What do you want with me?" I finally ask.

"Think about what has happened to both of us... Middle-school bullies and frat guys are cut from the same cloth."

Even though Ryan has been a good friend, I'm *nothing* like the person that he is exhibiting to me now. He thinks that, because of my history of being bullied by Vinyl and his friends, I will be an easy recruit for his twisted plan. But he's wrong. My immediate concern is with the resort and making sure people get out of this mess alive.

The island is getting further away every second, and I glance down at the dark water as it churns away from the bow. The water that we're in is not that deep. If I can swim out of the channel and toward the shore Ryan wouldn't be able to follow in the boat. The water will be too shallow.

I reach up and wrap my hand around the USB and yank as hard as I can. The force pulls Ryan's neck, but the small chain snaps.

With the chain and USB in my grasp, I take a deep breath and jump in the ocean. My body goes under, and I hold my breath. When I break the surface, I'm disoriented, but I see the boat and catch a quick glimpse of Ryan looking down at me. I don't have time to stare, and I turn around and begin swimming.

My ears are flooded with the sound of splashing water, but I can hear the steady hum of the boat's motor behind me. I hear it accelerating. I have to hurry.

Finally my feet are able brush the ocean

floor, and I'm able to stand so that my head is above water. The waves are tall, and I bob up and down. One of them knocks me over, and I get caught in the ocean's force until I'm eventually spit out on the shore. The delivering wave recedes behind me, and I get to my feet. I'm in such shallow water now that I'm able to stand steady on my feet, and I run.

Once I get further up the shore, I spin around to see where Ryan is. He's followed me and is letting the boat bottom out. He's not going to leave the island without what I have in my hand—the USB.

I take off running toward home.

CHAPTER TWENTY

THE FARMHOUSE IS covered in the thick, thorny vines. The plant is going after any living thing it can find, and the people I love are in the line of fire.

I reach my hand into the front pocket of my jeans to make sure I still have the USB drive, and I'm relieved that it's still there.

It's raining harder now, but my clothes are already soaked through with ocean water so it makes no difference. Hesitantly, I take a step onto the grass of the front lawn. The vines run across the yard and wrap around the columns of the front porch. Within the shadows there is constant movement from the vines, and the sight of it reminds me of hundreds of coiling snakes. I look over my shoulder just to make sure Ryan isn't right behind me. There's nobody there.

I move toward the house and climb the steps. I wrap my hand around the doorknob and turn. The door is locked, so I pound on it with my fist. "Dad!" I yell. "Mom!" But nobody comes to the door.

I spin around and see that the vines are closing in on me. I've got to break into the house, I realize. My eyes scan my surroundings. Mom always keeps the porch clean and empty. There's no rocking chair, planter, hanging basket, or anything else I could use to bust the window with.

The safety vest I'm wearing will work as a barrier between my arm and shattering glass. I take the vest off and hold it flat against the window pane. Then I bend my other arm and slam my elbow against the padding. The window shatters, and shards of glass scatter into the house onto the foyer floor.

I use the vest to cover the jagged glass at the bottom of the frame and climb inside. I know the vines will trail behind me through the bare window so I have to be quick.

Without power, the house is dark as a cave, but it doesn't hinder my progress. I know the layout of the rooms so well I could make my way around with my eyes closed. I turn the corner into the kitchen and realize I'm already too late.

From floor to ceiling, the kitchen is covered in vines that are stretched across the counter and over the center island. They run up all four walls and arch overhead like a canopy. The swinging door is standing open, and a thick mass of vines has already reached into the living room.

I back out of the kitchen and move

through the house in the opposite way. There's a half bath in the central hallway, and I pause at the threshold. Three battery-operated LED candles are on the vanity, and the flicker of the tiny bulbs fills the room with yellow light.

Dark blood is splattered across the tile floor. A tangle of vines is reaching up from the toilet and squirming around like the tentacles of some kind of alien invader. My earlier assumption that the vine in the lab must have come in through the drain on the floor is correct—the vines have breached the island's water and sewer pipes which will give them easy access to almost any building on the resort. If Dad, Mom, and Officer Wooley made it back to the house I know they are most likely hiding in the room that is the farthest away from any water or sewer line. My bedroom.

The hardwood floor creaks under my feet as I round the corner and face the ascending staircase that goes to the second floor. There's a trail of something dark leading up the steps, and I realize it's more blood. My stomach clenches, and I put my foot on the first step. I'm so afraid of what I'm going to find up there that my whole body is trembling as I climb the staircase.

At the top of the steps, the trail of blood takes a sharp turn to the right. At the opposite end of the hallway, the closed door to the bathroom is rattling. Similar to what was in the kitchen and the downstairs bath, I know the vines have come in through the sink, toilet, and shower drain. It's only a matter of time until they find a way out. I follow the blood all the way to the end of the hall where I stand in front of the closed door to my room.

The door is unlocked, and I push it inward. The room is lit with the horrible fluorescent glow from a battery-operated lantern that is sitting on top of my dresser. Mom, Kristen, and Officer Wooley are here. Wooley is sitting on the edge of the bed. Mom and Kristen are standing in front of her, and both of them turn to look at me. Their faces are smeared with dirt and grime; their clothes are ripped and torn. Mom is holding a long swath of white fabric, and Kristen has got what I recognize as a brown bottle of antiseptic in her hand.

I move closer to them and realize that Officer Wooley isn't wearing pants. Her bare legs are smeared with blood. There are deep lacerations across the front of both of her thighs. "What happened?" I ask.

"I sat down to pee...," Officer Wooley starts to explain and winces with pain.

I realize what she's saying—she was in

the downstairs bathroom, and the vines came up through the toilet. They wrapped themselves around her legs, and the thorns…

"It was like I was being cut into with a saw blade," Wooley continues.

Mom wraps the fabric around Wooley's right leg and pulls it tight. The officer cries out in agony.

"Where's Dad?" I ask.

Mom stops what she's doing and looks at me. "We haven't been able to find him." Her eyes are bloodshot from crying.

I take a moment to explain to the three of them what's going on—Ryan recruited David to write the code that's controlling the vines, Ryan murdered David out of fear that he would slip, and Brockley figured it all out and even had evidence. Now, I'm in possession of the USB that holds the computer program, and Ryan is coming after me.

Behind me, I hear the vines slapping at the glass panes on the window. I can only imagine what the outside of the house must look like. I go over there and peek through.

The vines that are covering the lawn are parting, creating a clear passageway. A figure emerges from the woods and starts moving along the path toward the house. It is Ryan.

After taking a few steps down the path, Ryan looks up at me and smiles.

"He's here," I say and spin away from the window. "He'll kill all of us to get what he wants." But I'm not going to let him get anywhere near any of them. I look at Officer Wooley. "Where's your gun?"

Officer Wooley points to a rumpled heap of clothing on the floor in the corner. I go over there. What I'm looking at is her pair of dark blue pants. The leather belt is still through the loops, and her holster is attached to the belt. I unsnap the button on the holster and pull the pistol free. It's the first time I've ever held a gun, but I'm confident I can use it. With the pistol in my hand, I stand up straight.

"Turn the safety off," Wooley says.

I flip the pistol over on its side and see a small button that I can push. I do.

The officer continues. "Now all you have to do is cock it and pull the trigger."

With the gun in my hand, I take a few seconds to study the way it works. I've seen enough movies and TV shows to have the basic gist of it. It's not complicated mechanics. Just cock, aim, and pull the trigger. I can do this. I swing open the bedroom door.

"There's only one shot left," Wooley says.

While I'm descending the stairs, I put my fingers into a small tear on the end of my right jacket sleeve and rip the fabric so that it hangs loose over my hand, hiding the pistol. If there's only one shot, I have to make it count. There's no room for a misfire. The gun needs to be out of sight until I'm one hundred percent positive I can hit my target.

Once I'm downstairs I open the front door, step outside, and slam the door closed behind me. It's still pouring rain. The open path through the vines leads all the way to where I am. Ryan is close, and it doesn't take long for him to reach the porch and climb the steps. We are standing face to face.

Ryan is dripping water onto the old wood floor. In the dark, he reminds me of a sea creature that has risen from the depths— something ancient that has come back to set things right. His dark brown hair hangs in clumps over his eyes. The buttons of his shirt have come undone.

"All you have to do is come with me to the mainland." He puts his hand on my shoulder. "With what's on that USB, we can start a new society. One that's good. It will be a new beginning."

The perfect world he wants would never

work. He's talking about killing millions of people to reach his idea of utopia. "No," I say. "I'm staying here."

Ryan nods his head, accepting my refusal of his crazy invitation. "Where's the USB then?"

I'm staring at him, but I don't say a word.

He moves his hand from my shoulder and hooks his fingers behind the leather cord that's looped around my neck. "You can either give it to me or I can take it."

When I don't respond, Ryan pulls the cord tighter into his fist and twists. The leather constricts around my neck, and I can feel it pressing into my skin. He continues to turn his hand, pulling the cord tighter. The airway in my throat is closing, and an uncontrollable gargling sound comes from my mouth. The veins in my temples are throbbing with blood. I know Ryan won't stop until he strangles me to death. Just like he did David Fiske.

Underneath the torn fabric of my jacket sleeve, I use my thumb to cock the pistol. While Ryan is trying to choke me, I raise my arm and put the end of the barrel flat against his forehead. Before he has time to fully comprehend what's going on, I pull the trigger.

The crack of the gunshot is earsplitting. Ryan's body falls backward, and his hand slips away from the leather cord. His body thumps onto the floor. The pressure on my neck finally comes loose, and I'm able to breathe.

CHAPTER TWENTY ONE

DAD DIDN'T MAKE it.

On the day of his funeral, the weather is perfect. There's not a cloud in the sky. We decide to bury him on the island in a biodegradable pod that has a small walnut tree planted over it. I know he would have liked the idea of becoming one with the tree.

The congregation is small. There's me, Kristen, Mom, Officer Wooley, Milton, Tyler, and all of the other people that worked with us on the island. Dad's friend, Loretta, came in from Trenton.

During the service, I notice a woman that I've never seen before. She looks faintly familiar, but I can't figure out how I recognize her. Then it hits me—she resembles Dad. She has the same nose, eyes, and dark hair that's beginning to turn gray. It's his sister. Aunt Sally.

People gather at our house following the service, and it's here that I meet Sally for the first time. She tells us that she is tired of spending her life in hiding, and she wants to get to know me and Mom.

While Sally is talking to Loretta, I run upstairs. The old copy of *The Island of Dr. Moreau* is still in my room, and I take it back to the kitchen where I give it to my aunt.

"Dad would have wanted you to have it," I tell her.

Sally smiles at the sight of the book, and I see tears forming in her eyes. "We loved this book when we were kids." She flips to the back where her name was written long ago in her childish attempt at cursive.

One Year Later…

MY STOMACH GROWLS.

I'm at work, sitting behind the computer where I just finished filling out a new order form. The last time I did this, the year before, I had no idea of the colossal nightmare the resort was about to go through.

After I shot Ryan and destroyed the USB drive, the sun finally pushed its way over the horizon, and the barge carrying our food supplies arrived. The barge's captain saw the destruction that was caused by the vines and immediately turned around to get help from the mainland.

I look at the clock hanging on the wall. Kristen is out of class and should be meeting me outside any minute now. The campus is within walking distance to an inlet that has a scattering of small restaurants and shops. That's where we're headed next. I click the SUBMIT button at the bottom of the screen and close the form.

After graduation, Kristen starting going to the closest college that's across the water. She's rooming with Tina in one of the dorms on campus, but we see each other almost every day. I'm going to school there too.

Mom and I still live on the island, but we have no immediate plans of reopening the resort. Instead, we both work on the mainland. Mom is the manager of an elite country club, and I work in the Food Services Office at the college.

I stand up and push my rolling office chair under the desk. After I clock out, I step outside. The day is warm and sunny. Kristen is already there. She's leaning against the brick wall and stands up straight when she sees me. She smiles and starts walking in my direction.

We meet midway. "I'm starving," I tell her and put my hand around hers.

The two of us walk along the sidewalk of the old city street. A smiling man wearing a fedora is moving toward us. He has a framed picture held under his arm. As we pass the man, I glance at the painting. It is one of Mom's—the one of the thistle. For the past several months, Mom's work has been featured in one of the nearby shops. It makes me happy to see that she sold one.

From there, Kristin and I make our way to the water where we walk along the shore hand in hand.

ACKNOWLEDGMENTS

Thank you to my wife, Natalie, for your continued support, Norma Gibson and Dan Paxton for reading the first "complete" version of *The Resort*, Charles Campbell for always lending an author shoulder to cry on, fellow SCWA members for your feedback on various pieces of the manuscript, and my awesome Beta Reading Team who took the time to read this story over and over again: Elizabeth Tankard, Toni Miller, and Sabrina Andrews.

About the Author

BRYCE GIBSON writes fiction that takes readers to charming and oftentimes sinister areas of The South. He lives in South Carolina with his wife and their dog.

To learn more, visit his website
BryceGibsonWriter.com

Made in the USA
Columbia, SC
29 March 2019